FORTY DAYS HAS SEPTEMBER

By
MILTON LESSER

I0541406

ARMCHAIR FICTION
PO Box 4369, Medford, Oregon 97501-0168

*For more information about Armchair Books and products, visit our
website at…*

www.armchairfiction.com

Or email us at…

armchairfiction@yahoo.com

AN EVICTION NOTICE FROM THE STARS...

That's what Earth was faced with. The creatures who had inhabited our planet eons ago were returning to reclaim their home, and mankind was going to be sent packing, literally, to another planet in another galaxy! But the human race was given one final chance. Her only hope lay with a tough ex-boxer who found himself in a battle of wits with the most beautiful dame he'd ever laid eyes on—a beautiful dame who underneath the glitter and gloss was the most ruthless she-devil the galaxy had ever known...

Milton Lesser was a constant presence in the sci-fi literature world of the 1950s, and he remains one of the genre's most underrated and under-appreciated authors. This novel, "Forty Days Has September," is smart, snappy, raw, yet stylish science fiction. Engrossing and enjoyable from start to finish, it is undoubtedly one of Lesser's very best tales.

FOR A COMPLETE SECOND NOVEL, TURN TO PAGE 101

CAST OF CHARACTERS

PAUL REARDON
He was a broke, unemployed ex-fighter, and he had a chance to work for the most gorgeous woman on the face of the planet.

HADMAN
To describe her as drop dead gorgeous was an understatement, and her power over men was unlike that of any Earthly woman.

DIUNIUN
He was purple and only about three feet tall, and in his hands lay the fate of all mankind and even the Earth itself.

ENRICO JOAQUIN
One of the most successful and influential businessmen in the Merryville area—until "she" came along.

LAURA HARRIS
Sharp, pert, and pretty, she didn't believe a word Reardon said, but wanted to tag along because she was "intrigued."

QUINN BERKELEY
He'd been the mayor of Merryville for a long time, slightly on the pompous side and a bit of a skirt-chaser.

PHIL
A dumb lout, a brutish thug with a .45 in his hand. All he wanted to do was point it in Reardon's direction and pull the trigger.

ANGUS McDOUGLE
He and Reardon were vying for the same job—and all he had to do was beat the daylights out of him!

CHAPTER ONE
A Most Unusual Interview

I STOOD in line with about a dozen other guys, and I felt foolish. They were of all sizes and shapes, but most of them were big. Me, I'm big too, six-foot-one and pushing two hundred pounds, but my stomach was grumbling ominously because I'd had exactly one doughnut and a cup of black coffee for breakfast. If I didn't get this job, I wouldn't have that much tomorrow morning.

Promptly at nine, the woman came in. She wore one of those severely tailored suits popular these days, but it didn't hide a thing. Tall and lithe, with green eyes and hair the color of rich red wine, she made us all stop our fidgeting and look at her.

And looking, we started to fidget all over again. She was like that.

"Good morning," she said, raking us over with those green eyes. "I'm Hadman. I'm supposed to do the staring, not you. Will you extend your right arms and flex the muscles, please?"

We all did what we were told, and I don't know about the others, but I felt foolish again. The woman came down the line, placing her hand over each extended biceps briefly, then moving on. She was very efficient. In a couple of minutes, she dismissed half a dozen unsatisfactory applicants who left the room, grumbling.

"You're all strong," Hadman told the rest of us, "but some of you might be muscle-bound, I don't want that." She dug into a desk drawer, brought out a length of rope, throwing it to the first man in line.

"Skip," she said.

"What say?"

"I said, skip. Skip rope."

Just like that, and he skipped. When the rope came to me, I did a good job of it. Before I'd decided that flashing leather could make a battered, unlovely hulk of your face, I'd been a club fighter, and rope work came naturally.

When we finished, Hadman sent all but two of us home. "Very well," she said. "You're hired. Will one hundred dollars per week be satisfactory?"

I looked at the other fellow, a gaunt, sandy-haired individual with big ears and a homely face. He was smiling.

"It'll be fine," I told the woman. "But what do we do?"

"I'll get to that. Let me finish. A hundred a week for one of you, a hundred and fifty for the other. Which one of you is stronger?"

"How in hell should I know, lady?" said the gaunt man, honestly enough.

"Well, I intend to find out. One of you will have to give orders to the other. I won't have you acting out of concert. Your first job is a simple one: I want you to fight."

"Who?" I said.

"Why, each other, of course. The stronger man gets the extra fifty dollars a week. Let's go now, start fighting."

I just stood there, open-mouthed. She couldn't be serious. My companion grinned. "I can't fight this man. I have nothing against him."

"That doesn't matter," Hadman assured him. "First place, I have to see who's stronger. Also, when I give an order I want you to obey it instantly, no questions asked. Now, fight. Remember, fifty dollars a week extra for the man who wins."

THE GAUNT man shook his head helplessly, lunging toward me and swinging half-heartedly with his right hand. I stepped back, and the blow barely brushed my forehead, more a slap than a punch.

"Hey!" I said. "You're not serious. You're not going to listen to her—"

"Hit him back," Hadman told me. "Don't just stand still."

"She's the boss," my companion said, swinging again. I caught his fist with my hand this time, pushing him away. I was feeling more ridiculous all the time. He'd swing, I'd duck away and wait for him to swing again. Hadman stood off in a corner yelling for us to fight.

Many a good street brawl starts that way, with a couple of guys pawing awkwardly at each other. Before you know it, they're not pawing any more but charging in lustily.

It was like that with us, and maybe in the backs of our minds someplace was the knowledge of an extra fifty bucks a week. Anyway, when I brought a left hook around the way it should be brought around, and when he caught it squarely on the jaw and shook it off without going down, I knew I had a fight on my hands.

We stood toe to toe and slugged for a while, leering recklessly like a couple of kids. Hadman cried her approval, and when the gaunt man almost put me down for the count with a good right cross that landed a shade too high on my cheek, I stopped feeling ridiculous.

I weaved away to catch my breath like old Jersey Joe, but the gaunt man didn't give me a chance. He waded in on top of me, pouring lefts and rights at my body. That was his mistake—he got too cocky and lowered his guard.

Splat! This time the left hook jarred him and I was lucky. I felt a couple of knuckles crunch and knew my left hand would be good for nothing but wiping blood away from my nose after that. I crossed the right from someplace below and behind my belt buckle, and that ended it. The gaunt man shot up stiff and straight like a ramrod and his eyes went glassy. He tottered for a moment, then fell backwards, crashing into a desk and upending a typewriter. He stopped only when he lay flat on the floor with no place else to fall.

HADMAN brought a glass of water from the cooler and sprinkled his face with it. Soon he was sitting up groggily, but he didn't try to stand. His smile was rueful.

Hadman turned to me. "You get the one-fifty," she said. "That was a lovely demonstration." She patted my shoulder like you might pat a horse after it had run a race.

I felt like hell. My left hand ached, and I could tell it was swelling. My nose was bleeding and I had a cut over one of my eyes. "I'm glad you think it was lovely," I told her. "I think you're nuts."

"Don't you want the job?"

"Damned right I want it. But I still think you're nuts."

She shrugged. "You can think what you want as long as you're prepared to obey me to the letter. Are you?"

"For a hundred and fifty bucks? Sure. Only, what do we do?"

"I'll let you know. According to his application, the man on the floor is Angus McDougle. You're Paul Reardon. Angus—Paul."

I stuck out a hand and helped Angus to his feet. "Hello, Angus. I'm sorry—"

"What for? It was a fair fight, so forget it." For some reason, we both were embarrassed. That's something I learned later: all men are a little embarrassed in front of Hadman. She's too beautiful.

Now she began counting off orders on her fingers. "First, you get a week's pay in advance. I want both of you to get some decent clothing. What you're wearing is a little torn just now. Second, you can have a good meal, say goodbye to friends, anything you want. We're leaving New York tonight.

Third, you're due at LaGuardia Airfield at three this afternoon. I'll meet you then."

She turned her back and busied herself at one of the desks. I looked at Angus. Angus looked at me, and we headed for the door after Hadman gave us a thick roll of fresh new bills.

On our way out we bumped into a man wearing a dignified gray business suit. "Officer of the building," he muttered. "What's all the commotion in here?"

I thumbed him toward Hadman. "Ask the boss, Mister." I didn't doubt in the slightest that Hadman would handle him effortlessly.

I GOT TO the general administration building at LaGuardia by two-thirty, and since Hadman neglected to specify any particular airline, I bought a newspaper and sat down to read it. After we'd cleaned up, purchased our clothing, and eaten in a good restaurant, Angus had gone to say goodbye to a girl he knew. So I got to the airport early.

I'm a little fed up with the international news. It appears like the Commies are trying to do all over again what Hitler and his gang tried to do a few years back. I lit a cigarette and skipped over the news section, but I don't think I'd have done that had I known then what this Hadman business was all about. Maybe I was lucky, because it gave me a few more hours of sanity.

Anyway, I leafed through the paper until I came to the personals column. Try it sometime. It's a good way to kill time. "Come home, George. Mother went back to reading and all is forgiven" or "Do you think chewing tobacco is old-fashioned? Try Dr. Peters' special to readers of this column" or "I'm looking for a real Florentine chess set. Any offers?"

You get the idea. But one ad was so peculiar that I did a double take and looked at it twice, then read it a third time to make sure my eyes weren't playing tricks. It said:

EARTHMEN, YOU'RE EVICTED!

This notice is appearing today, August 15th, in every major newspaper in every major city in the world.

We, the Overlords, have come home. Unfortunately, you've done a botch job here on Earth, but still we're willing to give you transportation to anyplace in the Galaxy.

We mean business, and resistance would be futile. To see just how true this is, watch what happens within the next few weeks in what we have chosen as a typical city, Merryville, Kansas, U. S. A.

> *Signed, Diuniun,*
> *Overlord, Sector 13*

I was aware of someone leaning over my shoulder—Hadman.

"Well, I see you're a bit early, Paul. Been reading the announcement?"

"What announcement? Oh, you mean this crazy ad?"

"Yes, that's the one." She sat down and took a cigarette when I offered it, crossing her legs and looking prettier than ever in that attractive suit.

"Don't tell me you believe it?" I laughed.

She looked at me severely. "It isn't funny. Naturally I believe it, and I should know, Paul. Well, never mind—you'll see."

I felt like telling Hadman she was crazy again, but when Hadman looks at you a certain way with those cold green eyes, you don't tell her anything of the sort. It unsettles you, makes you nervous, or at times it makes you feel like the racehorse that just won. It's all according to Hadman's mood.

Angus found us at 3:05, and Hadman scowled at him for being five minutes late. It was funny. Angus actually cringed.

"It won't happen again," he assured her, and I think he meant it. "My cab got tied up in traffic. Then there was the matter of a pretty girl who didn't want to see me leave—"

"That's over and done with," Hadman said, "From now on, you and Paul are my bodyguards. Nothing else counts, not even your private lives. Shall we go?"

Bodyguards. Then that was it. But what on earth did Hadman have to fear? A rich, eccentric dame—could that be all there was to it?

"Where are we going?" Angus wanted to know.

"A small city in Kansas," said Hadman. "Name of Merryville," She didn't bat an eyelash when I peered at the fantastic advertisement again.

Merryville, Kansas. Funny how the pieces of a puzzle can fit together so readily but still yield nothing that makes sense...

HADMAN took Merryville by storm. In that first hectic week, I began to see just why she might need a couple of bodyguards, and more than once I almost wanted to get the hell off her payroll while the getting was good.

We got to Merryville on a Wednesday, and on Thursday afternoon we paid a visit to Twin Oaks Inn, the town's only nightclub, which turned out to be more a glorified roadhouse than anything else.

A couple of flunkies were swabbing down the dance floor for the night's activities. Off to the left, a girl in slacks, looking a little faded and old without makeup, was pecking away at a tiny piano and singing the lyrics of a popular song, tuning up for the evening. Three or four men stood at the bar drinking beer, and the barman was wiping down the stained oak surface with a big dirty dishcloth.

I leaned my elbows on the bar and ordered a beer. Angus stood with his arms folded across his chest and Hadman said: "Who owns this place?"

Everyone turned to look, at her. They must have liked what they saw, because they kept on staring.

"I said, who owns this place?"

The bar man, a scrawny guy with a sallow face and a long crooked nose, said: "Name of Joaquin, Enrico de San Joaquin. Everyone calls him Joker, but not to his face. He owns a lot of things besides this here nightclub, and he ain't here now. You want a beer too?"

"No. I would like to meet Mr. Joaquin."

"You're looking at him now," someone said. The voice was quiet, cultured, but it was hard around the edges. The man stood in a doorway off to the right of the bar. He wore a white linen suit, very expensive and very clean, and his face above it was handsome in a dark swarthy way. "I'm Joaquin, Miss...uh..."

"Hadman."

"Hadman. An odd name. Is that your first or last? Is it Hadman something, or Miss Hadman?"

"Just Hadman. My friends and I would like to see you, in private."

JOAQUIN looked at Angus briefly, at me even more briefly, but his smoldering eyes stayed on Hadman a long time and he said, "Very well. Will you step this way?"

The office was big, with a huge marble-topped desk in front of the picture window. This Joaquin did all right for himself.

"So they call you Joker," Hadman observed.

Joaquin looked up quickly, but she met his eyes with an innocent smile, and he melted before it. Right there, Hadman wanted to show who was boss, and didn't come off second best.

Joaquin shrugged. "It's because of my propensity for gambling. I've always thought that if you let people call you something behind your back, they have you at a disadvantage. But it doesn't work that way at all, and sometimes it pays to have them think so. Now, what do you want?"

Hadman smiled. "Why, I want a job."

"What can you do?"

"Suppose you tell me, Joker. I can do a lot of things."

"Call me Enrico, please. Umm-mm." He looked her up and down carefully, trying to do it without heat. Her trim tanned calves below the bolero skirt, her supple waist, her high-arched breasts under the light summer blouse, her too-beautiful face. His eyes were very bright when he finished.

"Yes, a lot of things," he mused.

I've said that Hadman could make men nervous, but she did more than that to Joaquin. He struck me, anyway, as a lustful, passionate man who hid it all under a cool, unruffled surface. But it was all veneer and Hadman could strip it away like so much putty.

Joaquin came toward her, took her hand in his, and placed his other hand on her shoulder. Angus and I could have been on the moon. "Hadman…"

She was smiling without mirth. She stepped back. "Paul. Paul, come here."

I GOT BETWEEN them, feeling silly. Hadman was a big girl and she could take care of herself. Besides, she must have known what she was doing when she started this. But I said, "That's enough, Joaquin. You're getting too familiar, too soon."

I don't know what made me add those last two words, maybe it was just orneriness. But Hadman didn't like them.

Her brows arched and for a moment she looked like she was going to slap me.

Joaquin bowed slightly. He took a white handkerchief out and patted his forehead. The veneer returned. Only once after that did I see it fall away again, and then it was too late for Joaquin.

"I will dance," Hadman said.

Joaquin was all business again. "A dancer, eh? I should have known. Where did you study?"

"If I told you, it wouldn't mean anything. You've never heard of the place, Enrico. Do I get the job?"

"I'd like to see how you dance first, naturally."

Hadman's answer surprised me as much as it did Joaquin. "No," she said.

Joaquin frowned. "Did you say no?"

"That's what I said. It's tiring, Enrico, the way I dance. Twice an evening I will dance for your guests, but that's all. No rehearsals—ever. Now, do I get the job?"

"Yes," Joaquin nodded. "I think you will dance very well indeed. You go on tonight, at nine and at eleven-thirty." He sat down and poured drinks for all of us. I think his reply came as a shock to him.

THAT NIGHT, Twin Oaks was crowded. It was a hot August evening, and Merryville's richer set came for the air-conditioning and the cooling drinks. They got much more than they bargained for...

I don't think Joaquin ever knew what my relationship with Hadman was, nor Angus. He didn't fraternize with us often, but now he was proud of what he had done, and he stood with us at the bar, chatting.

"You'll have to see her gown to believe it," he told us. "I had it flown in all the way from Chicago. Beautiful. I predict that Hadman will be a hit in it."

Angus smiled. "She will," he said. "I know."

I told him, "She'd better be. Joaquin has a big crowd on hand." Joaquin looked just a little nervous.

At nine, the lights went out and a single white spotlight caught the dance floor. Joaquin strode into it, looking very trim and confident. "I'm proud to present something new to Twin Oaks," he said. "From the mysterious East, the exotic Hadman."

That was all and a fanfare followed his little speech.

"What will your band play?" Angus hissed to Joaquin.

"I don't know," he admitted. "Hadman said she'd speak to them."

As it turned out, the band played nothing. There was only silence. A mutter here and there in the crowd, a cough, a shuffling of feet. And that was all.

Hadman floated into the spotlight.

She didn't wear any exotic Eastern gown. She wore her bolero skirt and summery blouse. Her wine-red hair flowed free to her shoulders, and framed by it her face was very white.

I couldn't see Joaquin's face clearly in the darkness except for his gleaming white teeth. He mumbled under his breath, "Where the devil is the gown? Five hundred dollars…"

Hadman didn't need it.

She danced.

For the lovers of all that is artistic and graceful in dancing, she was Salome and Pavlova wrapped into one, and the liquid grace of her motions was all the more wonderful because there was no music to distract.

For every man in the audience she was everything he ever wanted. For some a hot-blooded savage whose body could coil and uncoil impossibly, curling around their hearts and squeezing with the passion of every primitive mating dance there ever was, and then letting go with a suddenness that left them gasping. For others a lover both cruel and tender, who one moment would crouch demurely, a supplicant, and the next would pirouette cruelly away, demanding more than they would give. For others a wife, fetching pipe and slippers with her motions, giving in a few brief moments more than any man could expect from his wife.

She was mother and sister too, for the women, and then all the passion was gone from her dance. She was tranquil and kind and everyone loved her.

At the last moment, Satan's mate returned, luring and mocking the men, weaving in and out among the tables, offering them everything and giving them nothing.

And then she was gone. She simply stepped out of the spotlight and disappeared.

Twin Oaks shook with applause, with roaring, with stamping of feet. In that brief five minutes Hadman had been everything to everyone, and it was another ten minutes before the crowd settled back. They did not even cry for an encore; anything else would have been superfluous.

Joaquin spoke into a microphone after the lights went on. "The drinks are on the house," he declared, "in honor of Hadman!"

I lit a cigarette with trembling fingers, and Joaquin was at my side. "Gawd," he said softly, so softly that he might have been speaking to himself. "What is she?"

It was a good question.

CHAPTER TWO
Merryville Goes Crazy

IN THE early hours of the next morning, we found out that Hadman was as good a gambler as she was a dancer. Joaquin had a nightly poker game in his office, strictly by invitation and it could have been a tear sheet from Merryville's society page.

The big cigar-smoking man with the very red cheeks was Merryville's mayor, Quinn Berkeley. He didn't pay too much attention to his cards; he was too busy looking at Hadman. To his left sat Joaquin, and beyond him was Sam Springer, a small, dissipated fellow who owned the city's one big hotel, the Merryville.

Springer's partner in the hotel business was a sour man of middle age who looked like he was perpetually sucking on a lemon, name of Purness, I think. There were two other men whose names I forget. But both of them, as I remember it, were in the real-estate business.

The seventh player was Hadman.

Of the other half dozen, only Springer and Purness came late, too late to have seen Hadman dance either at nine or at eleven-thirty.

Angus and I had an easy night of it, lolling about the room, watching the poker game, and helping ourselves to Joaquin's good stock of liquor. But a couple of Joaquin's flunkies came in and out too, and I don't believe they liked us one bit.

Mayor Quinn Berkeley apologized every time he stayed in a pot with Hadman. He apologized even more when he raised her—but he really didn't have to. Hadman didn't lose a single hand in which she remained for the final card. That became pretty clear as the game moved along. The room filled with smoke in spite of the air-conditioning, voices grew louder as more liquor was consumed. But by the time two hours had passed, only Springer and Purness stuck it out if Hadman was around for the final card.

AND HADMAN was doing just fine. They played two dollars and five, and that could add up to a lot of money when you win better than one pot out of three in a seven-man game. Springer and Purness were the heavy losers, and once Purness said in his sour voice: "I don't understand how she does it. I'd almost say—"

"Beginner's luck," Mayor Berkeley's voice boomed. "Wait till Miss Hadman's been in our poker club for a while. She'll calm down. They all do, I always say."

"Well," Purness continued doggedly. "I'd swear that something—"

"I'll bet one thing," Berkeley said, putting down his cigar and laughing. "Miss Hadman's the prettiest addition to our poker club we've ever had. Yes sir, the prettiest!"

"That isn't hard to believe," Springer said dryly, "since she's the only woman."

Hadman stretched languidly. "What were you going to say you'd swear, Mr. Purness?"

Everyone looked at sour-faced Purness, and Purness got nervous. Damn Hadman, she was goading him on!

"Let's forget about it, eh?"

"Why?" Joaquin demanded. "The lady's calling your bluff, Purness. Are you going to answer?"

Purness shook his head. "Let's play poker, huh?"

But the next hand did it. Berkeley folded after the first three cards had been dealt in seven-card stud. Joaquin tossed in a couple of blue chips; Springer rode along. But Purness made it five, scowling when Hadman and Joaquin were the only callers.

Angus whispered to me, "I think he's got trips. Sure has a cruddy poker-face, Paul."

I grunted something, then watched Joaquin dealing the next card. Purness got a pair of ladies up, and he pushed five chips forward, smugly.

"Don't tell me he's got four of a kind," I grinned at Angus.

Hadman, with a two and a five up, raised him.

Joaquin turned his cards over, grumbling something about being caught in the middle.

Purness upped it again, and Hadman merely called. The final two cards showed nothing in either hand and Hadman merely called Purness' bet. A moment later, he smiled when they were dealt the seventh card down. But his face still looked sour.

"Want to take the limit off this one?" he asked.

"What do you mean?" Hadman answered with a question of her own.

"Forget this penny-ante stuff—bet what we want. Just this once?"

"All right."

Purness forgot about his chips, reached into his billfold and took out a stack of money. He counted it out, in twenties, shoved it toward the center of the table. "Five hundred dollars," he said. "You either call or get out, Miss Hadman."

SHE SMILED sweetly. "I'll do neither. I'll raise you five hundred and make it a thousand. That is, if Joker will advance me the money."

Joaquin's face crimsoned slightly, but he gave her the money. Everyone was very still when Purness raised again, to fifteen hundred. Joaquin sighed and handed her the money when Hadman just called.

Purness turned his closed cards face up slowly. "Count 'em," he said. "Four. Four ladies." He began to reach for the money.

"Very pretty," said Hadman. She laid out a baby straight flush, one-two-three-four-five of hearts. "But not pretty enough, is it?"

Purness just sat there, the muscles of his jaw working. Finally, he said: "I think you cheated, Miss. I don't know how, but I think you did. It's not the money, it's the principle of the thing. I demand—"

Hadman's face got very white. She pointed a finger at Purness, held it there unwavering, inches from his nose. But she turned her face to me.

"Kill him, Paul!"

"W—what?" I stammered.

Everyone began to laugh, and Mayor Quinn Berkeley said: "Congratulations, Miss Hadman. You sure have a way to break the tension over a hot poker game. Kill him, hah-hah. That's good! Kill him…"

Hadman stood up. She seemed confused. "Never mind, Paul. Forget that order. I'm…mixed up. I didn't realize…" She pushed all her money and chips to the center of the table. "Here," she said. "You can all take what you lost. I've had an unfair advantage."

"Hah-hah…that's good, too," laughed Mayor Berkeley.

"I'm serious. Go ahead, take it. I was just having a little fun."

"No. You won it fairly," Joaquin told her. "I think the men here would know if any cheating had been done. I'd be the first to spot it."

"Think so?" Hadman smiled. "Here, take the deck. Now, mix it. Yes, that's right. Place it face down on the table. All right, turn over the first card. It's the seven of diamonds."

It was.

"The next one is the king of clubs."

Right on the nose.

"Three of spades."

Hadman went through the deck, and didn't miss once.

NO ONE SAID anything when she finished. They all left the room, saying goodnight to Joaquin, nodding to Hadman. They all looked badly frightened. Even a college sophomore at an all-night poker session would have been able to tell that those cards were not marked in any way.

Joaquin lit a cigarette, crushing it out after the first puff. "How did you do that, Hadman? This will surprise you, but I am a religious man. I have seen things that are miraculous and that I could attribute to God, perhaps. But not this, this is not God's work. How…"

Joaquin was dead serious. Hot-tempered within, coated with an unruffled veneer on the outside, he yet had a religious core someplace in his makeup. Hadman had a way of dwarfing all around her, but still, this Joaquin could be an intensely interesting man. And now he was badly shaken, although he didn't show it.

Hadman shrugged. There were only the four of us in the room: Joaquin, Angus, myself, and Hadman. "Incredible things will be happening soon in Merryville," she told us. "This is part of it, but just a small part, because while my knowledge and abilities may be God-like to you, they are puny and inconsequential by another standard."

"You speak in riddles," Joaquin said. "What about that trick with the cards?"

"It wasn't a trick. Consider, Enrico: you can see colors, a dog can only see black and white. I can see as much more than you, as you can see more than a dog. Your scientists call it extrasensory perception—this ability to see with a sixth sense, which has no bodily organ. Good night."

And she walked from the room, as quickly as that. Joaquin stared after her, and we left him that way, Angus and I, as we followed Hadman out to the taxi stand and then back to our hotel.

Angus and I shared a room together, and soon I heard him snoring. I couldn't sleep. I listened to the radio for a time, heard a local news commentator have some fun with the announcement in the newspapers that told of an eviction notice and strange things in store for Merryville.

I didn't think it was funny at all. You'd have to see Hadman's dance to believe it, but it was something no human woman could duplicate. Then, there was her command to kill Purness. She hadn't been kidding. I could sense that. She had merely forgotten where she was and what laws govern this world of ours, and it was almost as if she had given me a flyswatter and said to me, "Crush that pest, it annoys me."

Worst of all was the card trick. I didn't even try to figure that one out.

MARTIAL LAW came to Merryville on Monday.

The trouble started with a little five-year-old kid named Harold Peters. Harold, the *Merryville Gazette* related, liked to play near the attic window of his folks' home. Tragedy should have struck Merryville on Friday—and didn't.

Harold fell out of the window.

His mother saw him fall, the *Gazette* reporter wrote. So did his big sister who, some insist, actually pushed him.

Harold tumbled from the window in broad daylight. His mother screamed and half a dozen passersby looked up in time to see Harold spinning gently in the air. He floated as serenely as a feather, and when a gust of wind whisked in from East Main Street, it lofted Harold skyward.

Apparently he liked his impossible ride. People heard him laughing as his body ascended, becoming a tiny dot against the blue sky.

Then Harold dropped down slowly, spinning end over end like a boy-shaped balloon. He alighted on his backside with a gentle bump and scurried off to play with his sister. His mother relates that he wanted to try the stunt all over again, but she locked the window.

I don't know why, but I associated the whole story with Hadman. I knocked on her hotel room door and barged in, the newspaper clutched in my hand. Hadman pulled a dressing gown around herself as I entered, and I got a quick flash of long, beautiful thighs. Hadman's just a woman to me, if a gorgeous one, and so while I frankly admired what I had seen, Angus, I think, would have been half-delirious with this vision of a goddess emerging from her bath. That would cause a lot of grief, later.

"Good afternoon," Hadman greeted me. "I didn't send for you, Paul."

"Sorry," I smiled, "but I'm not a puppet. Maybe I'll come running when you pull the strings, because you're paying me. Meanwhile, I have a mind of my own."

She shrugged prettily. "Well, I guess it's a good thing you have some initiative, at that. Now, what's on this mind of yours?"

"Plenty," I handed her the newspaper, pointing to the article about Harold and his exploits. "What do you know about that?"

She read in silence, then looked up. "What makes you think I should know anything about it?"

FORTY DAYS HAS SEPTEMBER

Her attitude struck me as being more important than her meaningless evasion. She didn't seem surprised in the slightest. I said, "Answer the question."

"Well," she lit a cigarette. "I know that you have something here that you call a law of gravity. A body will fall downward at eight feet per second the first second, accelerating eight feet per second each additional second. Right?"

I said I thought so.

"It's a stupid law, like all of your so-called 'natural' laws. It's based purely on what you see, with mathematics dragged in by the shirttails to make it convincing. Because you observe that bodies fall that way a million times running, you assume it will happen the million-and-first time. Brother, as your song says, it ain't necessarily so…"

I MUST HAVE scowled, because Hadman said I looked silly. I guess my face isn't made for scowling. "Look," I told her, "you're still not answering the question. Do you know anything about this?"

"If you put it that way, no. But I can make a very good guess. Remember something about Merryville's selection as a typical city? What happens here will show that any resistance to the Overlords' commands would be futile. Well, things are starting to happen. And that's all I know, Paul.

"Now, will you get out of here and let me dress? I have to see Joaquin in an hour, and I'll want you and Angus to come with me."

She turned her back and began to strip off the robe, cocksure in her knowledge that I'd leave the room because she had dismissed me.

She could go just so far playing the goddess. I stood there whistling. Hadman flung herself around angrily, belting the robe again. Her face had taken on a tint or two from her wine-red hair.

"Get out!" she screamed.

Hadman was boss, yes, because she paid me. But not boss to that extent. "Say please," I told her.

I'll admit this about Hadman, not until the very end of the Merryville adventure did she lose her temper. She ran toward me now and I thought for a moment she'd rake those long gleaming nails over my cheeks.

Instead, she threw her arms around me and kissed me.

Hadman felt like she looked—warm, vibrant, alive. The kiss was magnificent, that's the only word I know that can do it justice.

She pushed herself away from me slowly. "Now will you go, Paul? There's a darling. And if you're good, I might do that with you again sometime."

I went. My knees felt weak and I garbled "see you" in a croaking voice. Hadman had a way of treating you like something less than human, this time like a faithful lapdog. And it worked.

Round one for Hadman, and almost by a knockout.

"WHAT THE hell's the matter with you?" Angus demanded as we were eating lunch in the hotel coffee shop. "You sure look confused."

I asked him if he knew about the kid, Harold Peters. No, he hadn't heard, but newspapers certainly could exaggerate things. Besides, what did that have to do with Hadman?

Right or wrong, I decided to make a clean breast of it. Angus and I were in this thing together, and I related the incidents with Hadman. "Quite a kiss," I finished. "Wow!"

He looked hurt. "You shouldn't have kissed her, Paul."

"You didn't hear straight. I didn't kiss Hadman, she kissed me. She started it, but I sure as heck liked it."

"How can I say it, Paul? I mean, I think Hadman is above that kind of stuff, as far above it as you're above the binary fission of an amoeba."

Lord, he was smitten with the goddess Hadman! "You're missing a trick," I told him. "Look at it this way. Hadman wants that. She can lead you around by a nose-ring, Angus. No, let me finish. She couldn't do that with me today, so she tried the kiss. I'd be a liar if I said it failed.

"What about the rest of them here in Merryville? After the dance she had them eating out of her hand. And Joaquin, I think Joaquin both fears her and loves her. Also, she took care of all those big wigs at the poker game. She called Purness' bluff, and he backed out. She returned all her winnings, and, by the time they said goodnight, everyone from Merryville's mayor to its two important real estate magnates were scared stiff.

"Hadman's taking over this town, Angus. Don't ask me why, but that's what she's doing."

"I don't—" Angus began, only he never got the rest of it out. Someone started screaming.

A sluggish molten river flowed into the restaurant from under the swinging doors that led to the kitchen. It hissed and smoked, cutting a channel for itself in the wooden floor. Bubbling and seething, it oozed forward like a flow of lava.

Out through the swinging doors, a cook came running, his big white hat falling into the burning stream. He skirted it ponderously with his huge bulk, shouting: "Cripes! I don't know. I quit. I'm finished. *Pfft!* I light my stove and it melts. Yeah, melts and starts running off like a brook, burning everything in front of it—"

People ran from the coffee shop, waitresses, diners, everyone. I saw one shifty-eyed individual dig into the cash register with his hand and then disappear in the crowd.

With Angus, I was among the last to leave. I knelt for a moment near the stream, which by now had burned a channel completely through the floor and begun to drip down in big congealing drops to the basement. The stuff looked like molten iron and it was cooling fast. Ridiculously, I wanted to reach out and touch it. But Angus pulled me away.

THE FIRE department arrived simultaneously with the police, and the chief conferred with Purness, who wrung his hands together sadly. His scrawny partner, Sam Springer, assured the crowd that they had nothing to fear. The police confirmed this, because the stuff had burned itself out and had hardened into a dull, irregular mess of iron in the basement.

The fire department went home, but the police remained to ask questions. One of them approached me.

"People say you were about the last to leave, Mr. Rear—"

"Reardon. Paul Reardon. Yes, that's true."

"What was that gunk like?"

"Well, I thought it looked like metal, molten metal."

Sam Springer came over and joined us. "That's fantastic. Do you know how much heat you'd need to melt iron? Plenty—a couple of thousand degrees, I think."

Hadman's statement concerning our natural laws crossed my mind. If gravity could go haywire because there wasn't any valid law to begin with, how about the law that said iron must melt at such-and-such a temperature? I remembered a book I had read once. Some philosopher had gone off the deep end a couple of hundred years ago, declaring that all our scientific laws were unwarranted intuitive jumps—assumptions that might not hold water at all. What was his name? Home or Hume or something like that?

Two lab technicians from the police department settled it. They arrived a few minutes later, went down to the basement

27

and examined the stuff. They didn't look so good when they came out.

"It's iron," one of them said.

"Yeah." added his companion. "Iron all right. It turned molten, flowed into the coffee shop because the floor slopes one-point-five degrees. Mr. Springer, was there a stove along the left hand wall in the kitchen?"

Springer nodded. "Certainly. A big job with a dozen ranges. Why?"

"It's not there now. But what beats me is how anyone got it hot enough to melt without destroying the whole building. Besides, you'd need coke and hard coal and carbon and a lot of other things."

The cook scratched his bald head. "I turned on one range, that's all. The stove started to glow around the fire. Yeah, glow. Then it dripped and began to disappear, sort of like if you put a chunk of ice under hot water."

The police chief spread his hands out eloquently enough. "I give up," he admitted. "We'll have to tell Mayor Berkeley."

"Just like a chunk of ice under hot water," the cook said again when the reporters arrived.

THINGS GOT worse on Saturday. Three more children defied the law of gravity. One little girl who was not old enough to walk rose out of her playpen and paraded around on the ceiling before her parents could get her down. The *Gazette* lost no time in drawing a connection between gravity's failure to assert itself and stoves that melted away. "Strange things are happening in Merryville," Saturday's editorial began. I'd call that the journalistic understatement of a lifetime.

Is there a law that prevents stones from falling out of the sky? Not meteorites, but the common garden variety pelting down in brief showers, breaking windows and denting brand new cars? I guess there is, but the law concerning such things took a vacation eight times on Saturday.

Sunday's editorial declared that Merryville's twelve-man police force no longer could cope with the situation. Reports came in furiously. A man turned on his hose to water the lawn, and only water vapor came out. Tomatoes, which a farmer assured police were normal the night before, swelled to the size of over-ripe pumpkins on Sunday. An eight-year-old youth who lived in Harold Peter's neighborhood grew a long curly beard overnight. Next door, a frail little woman who through all the years of her marriage had been beaten by her husband, astounded people by single-handedly freeing a car that wallowed hubcap deep in the mud after Saturday night's rain. She told reporters she felt stronger than Superman; and proved it by sending her husband off to the hospital with a black eye and three broken ribs.

You get the idea. Hadman smiled smugly with each new report, and if she knew anything, she wouldn't say. Late Sunday afternoon I cornered her in her hotel room, and I said: "If you don't want to let the police in on what's happening, okay. But you're going to tell me if I have to force it out of you. I'm not kidding, Hadman."

"Silly Paul, I know you're not. But I also know you won't do a thing about it."

I'd been drinking. Maybe I shouldn't have done it, but I felt a little giddy. I put my hands on her shoulders and shook her. "Talk, dammit!"

The door opened behind me and Angus strode into the room. "What's going on?"

HADMAN BROKE loose and sat on the sofa, sighing. "I just told Paul he was fired, and he took it hard."

"That's a lie!"

Hadman turned to Angus. "Would I lie?"

"N—no," he said. "Say, I hope I'm not fired too."

"Of course not. You can stay as long as you want. But up to now you've had it pretty easy, haven't you. You'll have to work a little harder today. I want you to throw Paul out of here."

Angus blanched. I told him, "Well, what are you waiting for? Go ahead, throw me out."

He was game. He dove for me, cursing. Maybe I had been fooling around half-heartedly that day in New York, I don't know. But now I met Angus' wild charge with a tattoo of rights and lefts to the head, and sobbing, he fell back and landed on the floor.

I whirled around. "Better get another boy who can play your game tougher. Better—"

Hadman smiled sweetly, and I didn't get the idea until it was too late. I heard a noise behind me, spun just in time to see Angus, his face bloody and twisted in rage, leaping at me. His hand flashed up grasping a big ornate vase by its neck, and I tried to lunge away.

I almost made it. But the vase crashed against my left temple and I staggered, half-aware of the broken shards tumbling to the floor. I guess I must have joined them, because the plush green rug came up to meet me, and then all the lights in Merryville exploded inside my skull.

I awoke with a headache. I explored the side of my head with my fingers and they came away damp. Groping about for the light switch and snapping it on, I stumbled into the bathroom, realizing that someone had brought me back to my own room. But Angus wasn't here.

I splashed cold water on my face and reached into the medicine cabinet. I couldn't have been out long, because the iodine burned as I dabbed it on.

FORTY DAYS HAS SEPTEMBER

Back in the bedroom I found a bottle of Scotch, which Angus kept around, and I took a long pull from it. That made me feel a little better, but it didn't last. It was then that I saw the note.

Scrawled hurriedly, a woman's handwriting—Hadman's, I guessed.

Paul: I liked you. You could have been a good pet. You chose otherwise and I can't help that. You know too much, you tie too many things together, and I'm not yet ready for that. I still should like to see you live, Paul, because you really do amuse me. But this is a choice that you must make for yourself. I've given orders for you to be killed in Merryville, and you'd be surprised if you knew how many people work for me now. You can either get out of Merryville or die, Paul.

It was signed with the letter H.

HADMAN wouldn't joke. She meant it. My number was up in Merryville, and I didn't doubt in the slightest that she had enough cronies in town to get me ready for a long pine box. I frowned at myself in the mirror when I went to wash my face again, I said aloud, "Don't be a chump, Paul Reardon. You're no hero. Why don't you clear out of this burg?"

I shook my head to clear it. She had me talking to myself already. If I didn't watch out, I'd really go off my rocker.

I still felt all washed out. I showered, shaved, took a long nap, then dressed. It was getting late.

Downstairs at the snack bar I had a couple of hamburgers and a bottle of beer. Smiling, I charged it to Hadman. By the time I finished eating, the clock over the cash register said one A.M. and I decided to get the hell out of Merryville.

That was one o'clock, Monday morning. At one-thirty, the militia came to Merryville at the urgent request of its

31

mayor, Quinn Berkeley, rolling into town in regimental force, stringing barbed wire and posting sentries almost in less time than it takes to tell.

I guess I was too busy with my own thoughts to find anything strange about the number of soldiers on Main Street. Maybe if I'd looked carefully I'd have seen rifles and fixed bayonets. I don't know. Anyway, I planned to hit it out of town on the main road up north, walking until I could find a place to sleep, then trying my luck at hitchhiking in the morning.

It didn't work out that way at all. Where Main Street turns into Route 30, uniformed men had dug big holes into the ground and hammered fence posts into them. Coils of wire were stacked in neat piles.

A corporal stopped me, and this time I saw the fixed bayonet. "Where have you been, friend?" he demanded.

"Sleeping."

"Well, you missed the radio announcement. The Mayor cried to the governor, the governor sent in the National Guard. Merryville is under martial law—and no one can come in or leave the city until this mess is cleared up. That's what the lieutenant says, anyway. Say, maybe you can tell me what's going on? We G.I.'s heard rumors, but hell, you know the army…"

I tried two other roads with the same results. I cut across a field and ran into soldiers stringing wire. I told a taxi driver I'd give him fifty bucks to deposit me outside the city limits—not that I had fifty bucks. But he said we'd never get beyond the outskirts.

BY THREE-FORTY-FIVE I gave it up as a bad job and trudged wearily back to the hotel. The night clerk called after me as I stepped into the elevator. "Mr. McDougle changed to a single room, sir. Will you want one too?"

His words didn't register until I reached our floor, the seventh. When they did, I got careful. I edged up to the door and tried the knob. Not locked. If Angus changed his room, there must be reason…

Flat against the wall, I twisted the knob and pushed the door in. A loud report shattered the silence, and something splattered against the far wall of the corridor, digging a hole before it spent itself.

I took a quick look inside the room. On a chair facing the door, a smoking revolver was tied securely, a piece of string extending from the trigger to the inside of the doorknob. The muzzle pointed an unblinking eye right at the center of the doorway, where I should have been when I entered…"

People came out into the hall sleepily, rubbing their eyes, sniffing gunpowder and talking loudly about the explosion.

I ran to a fire exit and plunged downstairs, quick.

CHAPTER THREE
Diuniun

ALL NIGHT I walked the streets of Merryville aimlessly. A couple of times I found myself dodging from shadows and my heart did a mad dance inside my chest. It was a hell of a fix. I couldn't go to the police because they had nothing more to say about things in Merryville now that the army had come. But people would be gunning for me all over the city, unknown, unexpected people.

And I couldn't leave. It was almost funny. I tried a sleepy-eyed Private First Class who got me through the echelon as far as a captain. He listened politely to my story, then went into a tirade about cranks and crazy happenings and would I please go home to sleep.

I crossed Main Street and mingled with a little knot of citizens who had decided to spend the night outdoors in the interest of science. As one old cadger put it, "If anything takes place like what happened the last few days, I want to be awake to see it. You think maybe it's the Russians, young feller? Folks say maybe they have some new secret weapons because we have more atom bombs. I dunno—maybe they're trying 'em out in Merryville."

Five minutes after I left the crowd, I realized someone was following me. Just a shadow among shadows, but it flitted in and out among the patches of light shed by the lampposts.

When I stopped, it halted too, half a block away. I began sweating. A soldier marched by, fixed bayonet gleaming under a street light. He nodded curtly and told me to get indoors.

My palms were clammy and I started to run. The shadow ran with me, two or three dozen paces behind, I turned a corner gasping for breath, ran into a slouched figure, hat-brim drawn low over his face.

"Reardon!" he cried hoarsely, groping quickly at his belt. His hand came away with a knife.

The shadow turned the corner and joined us. Another man whose face in the half-darkness looked familiar. I thought it was one of Joaquin's flunkies.

I backed away from them warily, but the one with the knife commenced circling around behind me. I said. "Did Joaquin send you to kill me?"

"Ain't that cute? He wants to know if Joaquin sent us. Hey, Phil, did Joaquin send us?"

Phil was the man with the knife. He snarled, "Joaquin should only know. He'd have us flayed! Now, Reardon, don't make it hard, 'cause we got you—"

I stood, suddenly, with my back to a lamppost. Phil sauntered toward me, almost casually, running the fingers of his left hand over the knife. Then he lunged.

I DARTED around behind the lamppost, saw the blade flash in at me, then heard it clang metallically. The blade snapped off.

"Damn!" Phil swore.

His companion snickered. "You're careless. But don't worry, I got a shiv."

Phil half turned around when the other man spoke, and I used the side of my hand, judo-fashion, against the base of his jaw. He moaned and stumbled to his knees, and when the second man leaned toward me over his prone form, knife in hand, I kicked Phil in the face. He screamed out a mouthful of teeth and tumbled back against his companion.

I dove flat on my belly when the second man hurled his knife. It didn't miss my head by half a foot, hurtling by with an almost malicious sound.

Then I whirled and darted around the corner again. Only one man followed me; Phil had had enough for one night.

Ahead I heard a car engine idling. Sobbing in great lung-fulls of air, I stood in front of Merryville's post office. A mail truck idled near the curb and I could see a uniformed figure bending over one of those all-night outdoor boxes. I climbed into the truck, released the handbrake, and clutched into first gear. The postal employee yelled once and then lumbered after me, a big man holding a stack of letters against his chest.

I zoomed away down the street, watched the postman shaking his fist at me through the rear view mirror. I stuck my head out the window and cried, "Sorry!"

It was a mistake. Phil's friend had come up, and a shot shattered the fly-window a few inches from my nose. Now that his knife was gone, Joaquin's flunky had no choice but to use his gun, despite the fact that all the soldiers in Merryville might come running.

I left them both back there, and I think the pistol shot frightened the postal employee more than the theft of his truck. Still, I didn't have more than a few minutes of grace because this was a federal offense and all the soldiers in Merryville might be on my tail in short order.

All the way to the barrier at the end of Main Street, over and over again, one thought twisted through my brain. *They tried to kill me. They tried to kill me. Those cheap, no-good punks. Because a dame said so, they tried to kill me...*

IT'S FUNNY how your ideas can change. All night I had wanted only one thing—to get out of Merryville. Now I thought I could do it. Dawn threatened to come up any minute, but there still was plenty of darkness left. So I could ride right up to the barrier. I didn't think the soldiers would stop a postal truck.

But I was sore. I remember getting this way once before, when a buddy of mine had been killed during the war, but that's a long time ago. Now it was me, people wanted to kill me—and hell, I couldn't just stick my tail between my legs and run away, yelping, like a frightened puppy.

Twice they came at me with knives; they wanted to play mumbledy-peg with my rib-case. Twice they shot at me—with a booby trap and in person. I didn't think I'd be able to shave again if I ran away. I couldn't look at myself in the mirror...

They let me through the barrier, hardly asking a question. Only I didn't head up north to safety. Instead, I took the first cut-off—which led to Twin Oaks and Joaquin.

I pulled the truck up on the shoulder a good two miles from Twin Oaks and left it there. I chuckled. One more mystery for the militia to solve. Yes, strange things were happening in Merryville...

Birds twittered in their nests when I reached the roadhouse. The sun came up behind me, big and pink and beautiful. Almost I couldn't quite believe all the crazy things that had taken hold of Merryville.

The door wasn't locked, and a deserted Joaquin's dance floor looked as big as a gymnasium. I crossed it to the bar, realized my hands were trembling when I helped myself to some whiskey—

Someone cleared his throat behind me and I whirled— Joaquin! He stood there in a silken robe, smoking a cigarette.

"I'm an insomniac," he said. "I didn't know you were one, too, Mr., Reardon. It is Reardon, isn't it? One of Hadman's friends?"

"Ex-friends," I told him. "Joaquin, have you got about an hour?"

"We don't open for business until three this afternoon, so I have all the time in the world," He looked very tired.

"You couldn't sleep because of Hadman. Right?"

Smiling, he shrugged. "What do you want to tell me? If it's ex-friend and not friend, then maybe also it's ex-employee. If you're looking for a job here, the answer is no. We're all filled."

"That's not it," I said. I took down the bottle of Canadian, poured us each a stiff drink, and started to talk. I told him everything, and I knew I was taking a chance. But I couldn't go this thing alone, and I was willing to gamble on Joaquin. I didn't draw any connections between Hadman and the crazy eviction notice, nor between the notice and what had happened in Merryville. But I left the road wide open for Joaquin to draw his own connections, and he didn't strike me as a dodo.

WHEN I finished he lit another cigarette and frowned. "You're sure it was my men who tried to kill you?"

"Reasonably sure. It was dark, but I got a couple of close looks."

"So it goes," he sighed. "Reardon, let me tell you something. As near as a man can come to owning a town, I owned this little city of Merryville, until a few days ago. I control all the gambling, and there's a lot of it. The mayor is my friend, my very good friend. So is the bank president. So is the chief of police. Anyway, I owned the town. But I don't anymore."

"You're telling me!"

"Hadman does. In a few short days, she's undone what it took me a lifetime to do. I should hate her, eh Reardon? I should hate her guts, as the expression goes..."

I merely sat there, not saying anything.

"Well, I don't. I think I'm afraid of her, Reardon. No, don't be surprised. I'm not in the habit of babbling my life history to everyone I meet, but I had to talk to someone. And you're it. I fear her, Reardon. And…I love her…"

I took another drink. "Let's drop Hadman for a while. What about the rest of this stuff? What about the things that have been happening in Merryville?"

"What can I say, Reardon? I am a God-fearing man, despite everything else. If it is God's will—"

"Would you be willing to tie it in with the eviction notice?"

"Why not? It makes sense. Still, if it is God's will—"

"All right, let's forget that too—temporarily. Would you be willing to let me live here until this mess clears up? I don't know what I'll do, but I'll do something, Joaquin. Someone's got to, because I have a hunch this is a lot more important than just Merryville."

"How could you stay here? My men—"

"I didn't think you'd keep them after what they did."

"As a matter of fact, I won't. But consider, Reardon, if I say yes, I will let you remain here for as long as you want, both because I like you and I like what you are trying to do. And then Hadman comes along, lets me make love to her perhaps, and tells me to have you destroyed. What can I do? I want to be fair to you, Reardon. And Hadman's power over me I cannot at this time fight. I pray every night that I can be strong enough, but God doesn't hear me because I've been wicked all my life. So, what can I tell you?"

I got up. "Then it's no?"

"Reardon, Reardon—don't be bitter! *Madre de Dios*, I play the game fair with you! For your own good I will not permit you to stay here. A few hours, yes—but that's all. Bathe, rest, sleep if you want, have a meal—but by two o'clock this afternoon I want you out of here."

"All right," I said. "Okay. You know, when I came in here I thought I'd ram your teeth right down your throat if you refused. But now that you have, I can see your point. I think you're a square guy, Joaquin. And I'll take you up on that until two o'clock. Mostly I need some sleep."

"Fine. And perhaps…who knows…someday we will be able to chat about this and laugh over a good bottle of Cognac. Not the French type, Reardon, because the French are barbarians. But real Spanish Cognac. Someday, eh?"

TWO O'CLOCK came too soon. I slept most of the morning, got up to shave and shower at noon. Joaquin had a meal waiting—and what a meal! Oysters, roast duck, wild rice, & big slab of pie—and a lot of good white wine. When I finished, I felt better than I had in days.

Joaquin pumped my hand vigorously out in the big main room which was being prepared for the evening's festivities. "This is goodbye for now, Reardon—and good luck. *Vaya con Dios.*"

I'd walk all the way back to Merryville, a good three or four miles—and then, well, then I'd see.

But I didn't get half a mile. A big flashy convertible, top-down, roared up from the direction of town, and I got a quick glimpse of Hadman's wine-red hair as the car pulled to a stop a few dozen yards down the road.

"Paul!" she called. "Paul. Poor Paul. I really thought you had left Merryville after Joaquin's men failed last night." She sighed as she approached, the picture of innocence now, summer wind blowing her hair loosely, whipping her white skirt around her trim calves.

"I'm still here," I told her.

"And I take it you've been visiting with Joaquin. Well, no matter."

She opened her purse, reached in—and then she was pointing a little snub-nosed automatic in the general direction of my navel.

"It's a shame, Paul. If they couldn't do the job, I'll have to do it myself. You're going to die, you know. Right now. You have to."

She wasn't speaking to hear herself talk. Not Hadman. And I felt nearer to death at that moment than when Joaquin's two flunkies chased me.

"Why?" I asked. I wanted to stall for time. Anything.

"Why? That's a stupid question. You disobeyed me. Even if you didn't know what you know—which is very little—you'd have to die. You disobeyed me. You also tried to command me. You should have known you couldn't do that, Paul."

The damnedest part of it was that she still looked innocent. A car flashed by and she came close to me, linking her arm in mine, prodding my waist with the automatic and hiding it with her purse. She stepped away when the car disappeared around a bend.

"I'm sorry, Paul."

Her finger fascinated me. I saw it grow taut, beginning to tighten on the trigger. Hadman wouldn't pull it. I was sure of that. She'd squeeze the trigger like an expert, and she wouldn't miss. I'd be very dead.

DID YOU ever see a cloud come up suddenly out of a clear blue sky? One came now, swooping down like a vulture after carrion. Quick, just like that—and I'd seen enough crazy things in Merryville to accept this pretty much in stride. Hell, it saved my life.

One moment I stood there, facing Hadman and death on a dusty Midwestern road; the next—this cloud swooped low and enveloped me. Only then it wasn't a cloud any longer but a globe made of something like glass, only softer.

I stood inside it!

Hadman stared at me. She scowled. She stamped her foot. She looked very frustrated. I saw her lips moving but I couldn't hear what she said. I couldn't hear a thing.

The globe lifted. If I closed my eyes I couldn't tell, because I felt nothing. But the ground zoomed away under me with impossible speed. Hadman became a dot. The convertible became a dot. Then Joaquin's roadhouse swam into view—not much more than a dot itself.

Merryville was a little jewel in the bright sunshine, and then Merryville passed through the little dot stage before it too disappeared.

Patches of green and brown and sparkling blue started out big, then grew smaller, then disappeared. Vast formations of clouds were little puffballs of cotton.

Then dots.

Everything began to look like a map and I got scared. *Those big blue splotches over there... Count them... Five... The Great Lakes!*

I shuddered and huddled down in the bottom of my little globe. When I looked again the black cloud had returned and I couldn't see a thing. It was better that way.

When the cloud lifted, I found myself in a room with polished metal walls that curved in on one another overhead to form the ceiling. A window, ellipsoid in shape, broke the smooth surface to my left and I crossed the floor to it.

Far away, what looked like the rim of an inverted saucer glowed in the black sky. I blinked and then peered again. It was still there. I have seen fanciful pictures of what the Earth might look like from half a hundred thousand miles out in the depths of space.

This was no picture!

I gazed out on the crescent Earth, unthinkably far away.

"Beautiful, isn't it?"

The voice startled me. If each word somehow were plucked from a harp string, it might sound like that. I whirled to face the room with its curving metal walls.

A LITTLE man stood in the center of the floor, shifting his weight from one foot to the other. A man? Not really, because he wasn't three feet tall, including the pointed pink cap perched jauntily atop his head. His skin glowed a delicate purple; his eyes flashed the fires of a color alien to the rainbow. He smiled at me and his tongue darted over tiny pointed teeth.

"Yes," the mellow voice repeated, "it's beautiful. The most beautiful world in the Galaxy, and the Galaxy has more worlds than you have people on Earth. It's so beautiful that you can't blame us for wanting it back, can you?"

"I don't know what you're talking about."

He frowned petulantly. "I can't understand that. We placed the eviction notice in all your newspapers, yet you don't know what I mean. You Earthmen actually lie to each other at times, eh?"

I nodded, lighting a cigarette. The smoke surprised him, and he backed away a little, with short mincing steps. The words of the ridiculous announcement suddenly came back to me, and I said, "Don't tell me you're the Overlord of Sector 13? You're not Diuniun?"

"No other," he assured me. "I know, you thought a super-being would have super size. As you can see, that's not true, but we have powers, Reardon. Oh yes! For example, I speak your language by scanning it directly in the memory banks of your brain and selecting the correct words for my thoughts. In the same way I taught English to Hadman. Ah, Hadman—and therein lies the difficulty..."

"You're damn right," I said, "she wanted to shoot me." But I hardly heard my own words. A delicate little purple man—the Overlord. Could that somehow explain the universal legends of fairy folk, of elves, gnomes, goblins—of all the little creatures in Earth's folklore?

Diuniun smiled again. "Stop interrupting and let me talk. I had a reason for saving your life, Reardon. Ages ago, my people ruled the Earth. Stern duty carried my ancestors of that lost age away across the Galaxy. What it was doesn't matter, but the important thing is this: *we all had to go.*

"But we made provisions. We mutated one of the species of higher primates, and the result is man. Some of you we left here to keep the Earth ready for our return, others we took as servants. Hadman is such a one. But now our task at the other end of the Galaxy has concluded, and with our servants we have returned."

A SIMPLE story, just like that. And the elves were, in fact, the creators of mankind. Not the other way around in fancy.

If you saw Diuniun, you couldn't doubt his words. Small, elf-like, naive of face and puny of body, he yet carried with him an aura of power. Diuniun was the Overlord and all he said was truth; I knew that even as I listened.

He went on: "Now, we are back. Some among us feel it would be unfair to take your planet from you, since you've had thousands of years to build it up as your home, others disagree. We decided to let what we found determine the outcome. If you had done a good job here on Earth, we'd let you stay, finding for ourselves a second best world in the Galaxy. We are a fair people, Paul Reardon, and too old a race to be vindictive in any way. But if you had done a poor job on Earth—"

"Well?" I demanded breathlessly. Mellow harp tones or not, his next words might hold the fate of mankind...

"Earth is ugly! The small, petty ugliness does not matter, because even a man like your friend Joaquin has a lot of good in him. I refer to the big things. The Reds, Communists— what do you call them? —march with horror and destruction all over the world. I don't have to tell you that, because you know it better than I do. Think of your European cities of Vienna and Budapest, Paul Reardon. Do you see gay, happy waltzes, women dancing in the streets, men singing raucously but happily in beer gardens? You do not. In one city you see the threat of your Red dictators, in the other you already see the marching feet of the Communist militia. Is that not ugly?"

I told him about another would-be world conqueror named Adolph Hitler, and what the world had done to him. Brought together in their common wrath for the enemy, the people of the free world outside the Iron Curtain would not be denied, this also I told Diuniun. But I don't think I was convincing. I can feel pretty strongly about that, but I'm not a rah-rah boy. Maybe that's the trouble with too many of us.

"Listen," said Diuniun, "don't misunderstand. I'm on your side. I have argued with my peers against taking your world, because while with our superior science we could forge a home for ourselves elsewhere, although it would be difficult, you'd be completely unable to do any such thing. We'd deliver you elsewhere, to a world of your choice, and I suspect you'd all perish there in time. We wouldn't be able to lift a finger to help. That's one of the laws of my people. We don't interfere.

"STILL, EARTH is ugly. As Overlord of Sector 13—this sector of space, Paul Reardon—I must make the final decision. And I will do it fairly. It's hard for you to understand that, but fairness is an integral part of our makeup. We can act in no other way.

"The difficulties in Merryville were Hadman's idea. If we decide to evacuate your people and come home to Earth ourselves, Hadman will be the administrative officer in charge of evacuation of your cities and countries. Hence, one place—Merryville—encounters a sample of our science, which has come far enough along the evolutionary ladder to scoff at what you call natural laws. Hadman feels that will demonstrate the futility of any resistance. But Hadman, I think, enjoys it. She hates the other half of humanity, Paul Reardon, as do most of her people. They are jealous of their brothers living in a Garden of Eden—jealous of you.

"But I'm getting off the track. I want to be fair with you of Earth, Paul Reardon. I can be nothing but fair. But what my peers do not know, because every man's character is his own private business, is this: I am capricious, petulant; I like to act on a whim. And now I have such a whim, which is why I brought you here. I have watched you. I like you. You get ornery when someone tries to push you around, which is why Hadman almost destroyed you. Very well. My peers, the Overlords, look at humanity's history and say humanity is ugly because of Judas and Alexander, Timur Lenk and Genghis Kahn, Napoleon and Mussolini, Hitler and Stalin—"

A buzzing sound interrupted Diuniun, and he frowned. "What's this?" he muttered, more to himself than to me. "A scout ship back?" He walked to a wall and flicked a series of switches. There was a faint humming and a whole section of the wall fell away, revealing a long tunnel. I still didn't know where we were, but I had the impression of some monstrous ship that could travel the void of space like the Queen Elizabeth could ply the waters of the Atlantic.

Through the tunnel Hadman came striding!

"I came in my jet as soon as could," she told Diuniun angrily. "What do you mean by rescuing this man? I wanted him dead!"

"Temper," Diuniun advised her. "Sometimes, Hadman, you forget who is servant and who is Overlord."

Hadman—tall, lithe woman with strength in every line of her proud body; and Diuniun—tiny elf of a purple man with a quiet smile on his lips. Which was the servant, which the master?

"HE'S MINE," Hadman persisted. "Let me take him back to kill him on the Earth that sired him. Remember, you gave me a free hand in Merryville—with all the science that I wanted."

She laughed, the wine-red hair tumbling about her shoulders. "Come here and look at this." She led us to a section of the wall, which at her touch became a glowing amber screen.

"Something like your television," Diuniun explained to me. "Only, by comparison, that's crude stuff."

A room swam into view, full color and three-dimensional. Yes, our television was crude by comparison.

"...gravity, laws of nature, all that is fun," Hadman was saying. "But I've come up with something special this time, thanks to Diuniun's science. Mutation. Would you believe that thing once was a common, one-celled amoeba?"

The room in the screen was a laboratory, which Hadman identified as the biological lab of Merryville Teacher's College. I saw a man, a white-smocked laboratory technician, staring in horror at something that couldn't be seen yet, since the edge of the screen cut us off from it.

The technician turned and ran, but whatever it was had trapped him. He stood with his back to a great bank of machinery. He flung his hands over his head, all control gone, and his mouth hung open. He must have been screaming.

The thing came into view!

Large, much larger than the man—an amorphous mass of blueberry jelly, which even now threw out several pseudopods as it rolled forward. A giant amoeba, grown impossibly huge by science unknown to mankind. But that wasn't the worst of it. The thing had eyes!

A score of them, perhaps. Large, unblinking, they seemed to scrutinize the man. Then the pseudopods flashed out quickly and caught his ankles. Soon the man was immersed up to his knees, screaming, soundlessly.

The thing climbed, engulfing the man to his waist. Climbed... His legs became hazy, indistinct. Even as he stood there, screaming, he was being digested!

Hadman pressed a button, and the screen faded away. "They'll destroy it," she admitted. "But I have a whole bag of tricks up my sleeve, and by the time I'm finished they'll know who's boss."

I WANTED to call Hadman a fiend, to call her everything wicked and vile in the English language. But she wouldn't understand. She'd probably smile and talk about different standards. One half of the Overlords' experiment with their mutated primates could be chalked up as a failure. If Hadman were representative, the human servants of the Overlords were a cruel, self-centered, spoiled, Satanic people.

Diuniun waxed angry. "Play your game," he told Hadman. "Go ahead, play it! I still have faith in humanity, in the real humanity we left here on Earth an age ago."

"And the other Overlords chose you to decide the fate of Earth!" Hadman sneered. "You're weak, Diuniun. You're just decadent!"

He shrugged his tiny shoulders. "But *fair*, Hadman. And I was telling Reardon here that I have a whim—"

"You and your whims! I still remember that time on Korlay—"

"Shut...up," Diuniun said quietly. "Hadman, I will tolerate you because my peers wish it, but don't tax my patience. If I send you back across the Galaxy, and if we do take Earth, I can order you to remain on one of the worlds of the Fringe."

Hadman became pale and she shut up. I knew then. Diuniun, tiny purple Diuniun, was the Overlord. Hadman could flaunt her arrogance, and at times she might get away with it, but Diuniun was master.

"This I have decided," he said. "Earth will have a fair chance. For obvious reasons, we can't let the whole planet know what is going on, because we may yet simply go away. Thus, everything must be determined on a small scale, and Reardon is a good, typical Earthman. *Reardon, what would you do if I told you the fate of your people, the fate of all mankind, rested in your hands?*"

"I don't know what he'd do," Hadman scoffed. "But I'd laugh. I'd think that's swell, Diuniun—"

"I told you to shut up. I want you here because it's fair to permit both sides in on this. But Reardon, I mean that. The fate of humanity depends upon you. We will play a game to match Hadman's.

"Consider. The Overlords feel you've done a bad job not merely because of your Hitlers and Napoleons, but because the free people must always bicker amongst themselves at times of crisis. Because they never can act together the way intelligent beings should. All right. This is a time of crisis...you know that. Within the next few weeks, I must decide whether you Earthmen are to have your planet or not.

"It's up to you. Do you know the mythological character Hercules? He was given a series of labors to perform. Ahhh…you're nodding. I see that you know of him. Good. You too will be given your series of labors. But with a difference.

"First, Hadman will try to stop you. If you win, we Overlords don't get Earth, and that means Hadman doesn't get it either. Second, you must have companions in this venture. Remember, you must show action in a concerted, intelligent fashion. When I send you back to Earth, you are to stop the first three people you encounter, Reardon. No choice, and I will be watching you—the first three, whoever they are. They are your assistants. You can tell them what you want, everything or nothing. But the labors will be such that you cannot perform them alone. Three assistants, let the Fates decide who they are to be, and together with them you will shape the destiny of mankind.

"You will have ten days, Reardon, and a trio of labors. If you succeed, Earth is yours. If you fail, we take the planet. If you win, humanity will never know, because your ten days will be ten extra days, wiped forever from the racial memory. How many days does your month of September have? Thirty? Very well, this year it will contain forty days—the first ten are extra. Only you and Hadman will remember. For the rest of humanity, those ten days will be as nothing… Have you any questions, Reardon?"

I SAID NOTHING. Me, Paul Reardon. Just an ordinary guy who wanted to lead an ordinary life. Me, Paul Reardon—plucked out of the stream of life by a little purple creature who was something more than man and something less than God. Plucked out to play a game like old Hercules. Only this time all mankind shaped up as the stakes. Hercules and me. But I didn't feel much like Hercules just then…

"N—no questions," I managed.

"Hah!" Hadman snorted. "You win, Diuniun. I won't kill him. It will be more fun this way. See him? He's afraid— afraid. A lot of good he'll do for his people. Let him play your game. Let him. I'll watch, and I'll laugh. And we'll be landing on Earth before you know it."

"Perhaps," Diuniun told her. "But I still have faith in humanity, and in Reardon. Now I have things to do, so you can return in your scout ship, Hadman, and I'll send Reardon back to Merryville. Reardon?"

"Yes?" I felt giddy and I felt frightened, and Hadman was right. Why did Diuniun have to single me out? Anyone else, but why me?

"You will receive instructions for the first labor after you recruit your trio of aides. And now—goodbye and good luck!"

I stared dumbly. Hadman sauntered past, insolent, sure of herself. She whispered, "What a hero he's chosen! Paul, if I wanted to, I could make you forget the whole thing. I could make you love me, like Angus or Joaquin, and you'd come crawling on your knees to me, burning for my kisses. But I won't. Go ahead, play your game—but I'll see you dead before it succeeds. Remember, Diuniun said I could fight you at it."

She was gone, back through her tunnel and into her waiting scout ship.

Diuniun studied some charts. He hardly paid me any heed, but abruptly the black cloud seemed to grow in one corner of the room, and in a moment it had enveloped me. "Sort of like teleportation," Diuniun's voice came to me faintly. "No cloud and no globe, not really. Your mind fashions them to explain an otherwise complete impossibility. Clever device, the mind…"

CHAPTER FOUR
Hercules and Me

RAIN PELTED the streets of Merryville, a quick summer storm that sent everyone scurrying indoors. I guess I walked along Cedar Avenue furtively. I didn't want to meet anyone; I wouldn't know what to do. The first three, that's what Diuniun had told me; the first three would join me in this wild adventure. Or, as the little purple Overlord had put it, in this game.

For the winners, Earth.

Did you ever read a science-fiction magazine? More likely than not it contained a story of Armageddon, of man's final decisive battle against some cosmic doom. The stakes were the same, but the pawns in the game were different. Governments juggled resources to meet the threat; whole armies did battle with the hordes from space that rocketed Earthward to take our fair planet. One little city like Merryville didn't amount to much.

Now the real thing had come, and Earth plodded along in its age-old way, unknowing. Two billion people, all kinds of people in all kinds of places—and their fate would hinge on what took place in Merryville.

I wanted to curl up someplace, or maybe go on a roaring drunk. But that wouldn't be the answer. Diuniun had dealt the hand with finality while Hadman laughed derisively, and the next move was mine. I didn't know how to make it. I stood in the rain, feeling foolish, wishing I never had answered Hadman's ad, wishing I had not come to Merryville. September would find itself with a surplus of ten days this year, ten days that would be erased from the memory of man when Diuniun's game had played its course, ten days that could be the zenith or the nadir of all man's visions and dreams and hopes. I didn't think I was the man for the job...

High heels click-clacked on the pavement behind me, beating out a brisk tempo through the steady drumming of the rain. A girl's voice called out: "Hello there! You'll be drenched to the skin if you don't get in out of this rain, Mister. Want to share my umbrella?"

I shrugged inwardly. *Now as well as ever, and the first of my trio stood just behind me. I whirled and faced her.*

AFTER A WHILE, her face got red. I couldn't help it. I stared at her long and hard. But she didn't know why and she got the wrong idea. "Listen, Mister," she told me. "Don't think I'm picking you up or anything. I just felt sorry for you standing here in the rain, and my umbrella's big enough for two if we happen to be heading in the same direction. If those eyes are retractable like landing gears, please pull them back inside your head."

And then she started to smile. It must have been contagious, "because I felt a grin spreading over my own face. The girl had a pert, intelligent face and her rain slicker failed to hide a trim figure. Nothing like Hadman, of course, but she'd look mighty good on a tennis court or in a bathing suit.

"Honey," I said, "you just don't know how far we'll be going in the same direction in the next few weeks. How would you like to save the human race?"

She was still grinning. "They gave me a course in personality and behavior at Teacher's College, before I decided to become a secretary instead. But they never included anything like you."

"Tell you what, let me buy you a drink and explain. No—no, forget it, we might meet other people, and I want to get you all straightened out first. That's a nice big umbrella. How'd you like to walk with me for a while?"

She looked doubtful. "My mother warned me. She sure did. But Mr.—"

"Reardon. Call me Paul."

"Paul, I'll admit it. It's a brand new line and I've never heard it before. Okay. I'll walk with you because you intrigue me, but only because of that. If you're serious, you're crazy; and if you're joking, you have the craziest sense of humor I've ever bumped into."

I tucked her arm under mine and the umbrella's ribs brushed my head occasionally as we walked. Laura was a short girl, no more than five feet two or three. That's her name, Laura Harris.

Well, I told her. I didn't know how else to go about it. I told her everything I knew, quietly, without any dramatics. I started with Hadman, threw in the Merryville situation, and I began to feel better when I remembered Joaquin had believed me.

It failed to get a peep out of her, not until I finished. When I got to the part about Diuniun, Laura's mouth popped open a little, but she remained silent. When I lit a cigarette and walked for half a block without saying anything she turned around to face me.

"You certainly have a vivid imagination, Paul."

"That's all you'll say? Tell me that I'm nuts or something, or—"

"No. No, I won't do that. Here's the way I see it. You're a visiting fireman or some such thing in Merryville, and you're stuck here because the militia won't let you leave. You have no friends in town and you're lonely, so you want to strike up an acquaintance with a gal. I turn out to be a likely candidate, so you make with the wildest, most fantastic line since Eve told Adam all about the benefits of a certain tree. It's supposed to impress me, I guess."

"Does it?"

"No. Like, before, it just intrigues me. You want a date, I'll accept it. Two dates, ditto. I'll be frank, Paul. I want to see what makes you tick, but I'd like you to admit the whole thing was a gag. Don't get me wrong; peculiar things are happening in Merryville, but I can't swallow the answer you gave me."

I shrugged. "No gag. Honest, everything I said is the truth, as far as I know. You got a telephone number?"

She gave it to me and I watched her walk away through the rain. I'd keep it on tap and as soon as Diuniun's first labor came through to start the game, I'd call her. Meanwhile, World Savers Inc. still needed two members.

I began to whistle. Hell, if the other two turned out as easy as Laura, this selection of candidates might be a lark after all.

IT DIDN'T last. Number Two bumped into me on the corner of Cedar and 12th. By that time the rain had slowed to a drizzle. Number Two showed up in the person of Harold Purness, the sour-faced co-owner of the Merryville Hotel. His partner, Springer, had been very outspoken about the mysterious damage in the Merryville's coffee Shop, but Purness, who got the information second hand, took an even grimmer attitude. Someone wanted to put the Merryville out of business. Someone had thus started a campaign of terror, smacking in some unknown way of fantastic scientific powers.

"Who do you think that someone is?" I asked Purness.

"Reardon, I don't know. It's common knowledge that a lot of folks in Merryville would like to cut in on the hotel business. Mayor Quinn Berkeley, for one. Maybe some of the boys in the real estate gang. Even this Hadman dame. I don't know—say, you work for her!"

I shook my head. "Not any more, Purness, you've got your troubles, I've got mine, but I have a hunch the guy pulling the strings might turn out to be one and the same man. If I have a lead on your hotel man, shall I call you?"

A faint smile passed quickly over Purness' sour face. "You bet. Just call and I'll come running. In fact, you look like an able guy, Reardon. I'll make it worth your while—"

"Forget it. Maybe Hadman did cheat you that night at Twin Oaks, and since I was working for her, then I feel I owe you something. It's on the house, Purness, and you can bet you'll hear from me."

"Fine. Fine! Say, I have an appointment with Mayor Berkeley. Should be along any minute now. Maybe you'd like to stick around and get a line on what he says? Opposition in politics, you know. I was a candidate in the last election, and I wouldn't put it past Berkeley at all."

I STARTED to say no, because one man of Purness' ilk might be too much in this setup. I still knew nothing of Diuniun's game, but from what he had told me, cooperation seemed a keynote. I could just see Purness and Quinn Berkeley cooperating on anything short of mutual mayhem! But right then it looked like my participation in any game to save Earth for humanity might end in abortive failure because, swinging a cane jauntily, Mayor Quinn Berkeley stepped out of a car and joined us on our street corner.

Bluff, red-cheeked, he greeted Purness heartily enough, and when the hotel owner introduced me, Berkeley said: "Ah yes, Reardon! How are you, young man? Friend of Hadman, isn't it? Yes, how are you?"

"Here's something for the books," Purness said. "Reardon thinks he has a lead on that fire at the coffee shop."

"Is that so? Well, well... Good work, my boy. Like to join us for a round or two of drinks? Heh, heh...not much to do as a mayor these days, not when the army took everything over. Say, does that mean you have an angle on the rest of this stuff in Merryville?"

"I didn't say that," I told him. "But it could be. Have you seen Hadman recently?"

"Hadman? Why, no." His face got redder. I thought, *Reardon, maybe you should have been a psychologist. You'll have this pompous guy eating out of your hands in another minute.*

Aloud, I said, "That's funny. She's been asking about you. Seems she's taken a fancy to you, Mayor." *Reardon, you lie so well, you'll be believing it yourself soon.*

"Well, humph! She's a nice young thing, of course, but I've been so busy."

"The Mayor has a family," Purness explained, smiling. "They say his wife's maiden name must have been Xantippe. You know, wife of that old Greek, what's his name— Socrates. A shrew, a battle-ax."

"That's enough," Quinn Berkeley nearly shouted. "Reardon, next time Hadman asks after me, you let me know. Will you do that?"

"Sure thing, Your Honor."

"I thought you don't work for her now," said Purness.

"Umm-mm, I don't. But I see her. I'll let you know, sir."

"And don't forget about me," Purness pleaded. "If you get a line on that hotel thing, wild horses couldn't keep me away."

I told them both that I'd remember, and then I excused myself, watching them cross the street together, Berkeley with his big bear-like strides. Purness with the cautious gait of a conservative, pessimistic man.

AND THAT was it. World Savers Inc.—membership, four. Paul Reardon, President, ex-pugilist, good for nothing much more than going a few rounds with the ideal heavyweight aspirant. Vice-presidents: Laura Harris, a sharp young thing, pert and pretty, who didn't believe a word I said but wanted to tag along because my obvious insanity amused her. Harold Purness, sour, middle-aged businessman who had a bone to pick with the unknown agent of his difficulties. Quinn Berkeley, skirt-chasing mayor extraordinary, who wanted to show his wife, Purness, and their whole social set a thing or two by capturing the fancy of an exotic woman who had taken Merryville by storm.

Four people to save the world. I shuddered. Surely the Fates were joking…

Well, joking or not, they got serious on September 1st. I'd taken a room in a small boarding house, got a job driving a delivery truck for the department store in order to pay my rent. Several days fled by as September approached. A week.

And nothing.

I met Angus in town a couple of times, and while he acted aloof, he didn't get violent. Yes, Hadman was fine. No, Hadman didn't talk about me at all. But she seemed very busy with Joaquin, and that irritated Angus, who had a dispassionate crush on her if such a thing is possible. So Hadman had declared an armistice, calling her dogs off, at least until Diuniun started his game.

Merryville settled back and accepted a daily assortment of improbabilities while the army guarded and explored, investigated and theorized, all to no avail. Scientists descended on Merryville in droves. After a few days, sometimes after a few hours, most of them left town shaking their heads sadly. A cultist from Southern California claimed he could cure Merryville's ills and he was flown in air express, but he proved a fraud when twenty-four hours alleviated nothing but the cultist's obvious desire to see Merryville firsthand. They quietly sent him packing.

THURSDAY, September 1st. Nothing lurid, nothing melodramatic. I'd almost been expecting visions, or at least voices. But when I reached my room after the day's work, I simply found a letter waiting for me from Diuniun. That's what it said in the left-hand corner, where the return address belongs. Diuniun. His handwriting was perfect, but without style. Like those charts they have the kids copy in grade school, each letter formed simply and accurately, with no attempt at individuality. Evidently Diuniun had selected a composite sampling and his flawless script resulted.

I hesitated, staring fixedly at the envelope. Sometimes corny expressions have a way of asserting themselves in a situation that very definitely does not call for corn, and then they don't sound at all like cliches. Over and over, three words ran through my mind: *This is it...*

I lit a cigarette and inhaled so hard that it made me cough. I paced around the room, sat down for a moment on the studio couch, got up and snuffed out the cigarette, crossed to the window and watched a streetcar pull to a stop down at the corner, saw a fire engine hurtle up from the south, its siren wailing. Down the street three young soldiers flirted with a high-school girl, deciding after much debate to escort her home. A big Constellation droned high overhead.

Life went on in all its manifold ways. I wondered what they'd have done had they known...

I pulled Diuniun's message from its envelope.

To Paul Reardon, Greetings!

I observe that you have your assistants and now am ready. Of labors you shall have three, because you cannot be expected to duplicate the feats of the hero of ancient Hellas in ten short days.

Remember, I am watching: if you win through, clearly and decisively, the Earth is yours. If not, the Overlords will return to Earth with their servants, Hadman's people, and the planet will be for Earthmen no more! Hadman watches too. Have care…

Your first labor: Hercules had his Stables to clean. Very well, you will have your moral stables. You are to clean out gambling from the Twin Oaks Inn, either tranquilly or by force, as you wish. Remember, I am a man of whims, and for this labor my whim prefers the wiles and stealth of the fox to the brawn and sinew of the lion.

You have until midnight tomorrow evening. Diuniun

I GROANED inwardly, pouring myself a shot of whiskey. I liked Joaquin. Joaquin liked me. Unconsciously, I had counted on him for some support. But now the First Labor loomed before me, and Joaquin's gambling room in the rear of Twin Oaks was a major source of income. I could just see him acquiescing…

The police, the mayor, the big wheels of Merryville's social set, all stood strongly in favor of Joaquin's gaming and all Hadman had to do was utter one word against me and my goose would broil. She'd do it, too. Well, Hadman mustn't know. I'd keep the whole thing secret. I'd—

Something, I don't know what, tore at my mind. A tugging at every atom of my brain, a twisting, roaring pain surging through my skull—and laughter, Hadman's. Peal after peal of it mocking me.

Hadman, was she somehow reading my mind, gleaning from it the knowledge of Diuniun's First Labor? I tried to think of other things. I recited aloud. "Two times two is four, times two is eight, times two is sixteen, times two—"

Hadman's laughter swirled in my brain!

If she could run through a deck of cards and guess every one right, could she also read my thoughts like low-altitude skywriting? Could she strip my mind of its psychic barriers and remove what knowledge she sought? I struggled, swallowing great gulps of liquor straight from the bottle to cloud my brain. I fought."

It didn't work. I could almost feel Hadman's mental fingers plucking, seeking, taking... When her laughter faded from my head and disappeared, more mocking than ever, I knew she did not leave empty-handed.

"HELLO. THIS is Paul Reardon."

"Paul Reardon? Paul—oh! Hi." I hardly recognized the voice at the other end of the telephone wires, since I'd spoken with Laura Harris only once, and at that briefly. "How're the Labors coming along, Hercules? Or are you ready to forget all about that?"

"Forget nothing! The first one came through today, and it's bad." I told her about Joaquin's enterprises. "So, we'll have to clean out a different kind of stable. Laura, did you mean what you told me, that you'd tag along—"

"You bet. I still can't make you out, Paul, but I want to be around when things start to happen. Pick me up at seven? Swell."

Before I cut the connection, I told her, "There'll be two other people along, but they don't know anything about this Labors stuff. So don't mention it, huh?"

"Aha!" Laura cried with mock severity. "Resorting to a subterfuge, eh? Stooping to trickery—"

"Baby, I'd stop short of nothing if it means saving the Earth. Can't you get that through your head?"

She mumbled "oh" and said something about my being incorrigible, then she hung up.

I dialed Purness, told him I had a strong lead on the coffee shop affair, and would he meet me at Twin Oaks this evening? He'd be delighted. I called Quinn Berkeley, arranging a date for him with Hadman at Twin Oaks. He'd be happy to come, thank you. I chuckled softly. What would Hadman think of the idea?

By seven-thirty, Laura and I sat at our table in Twin Oaks, ordering our first drinks. "You're not very good company," the girl told me, smiling. "You've hardly said a word."

I said, "I was thinking..."

"What about?"

"The First Labor, of course. How the devil can we pull it off? Joaquin's gaming room opens at nine, remains opened until two. Only we've got to close it down," I snapped my fingers. "Just like that."

"The trouble with you, Paul Reardon is that you've got no imagination. Your little purple man compares this to Hercules' task with the Augean stables, right? Well, what did Hercules do? Those stables hadn't been cleaned in years, and maybe some little imaginative gal whispered something in old Hercules' ears, because he suddenly got a brainstorm. Know what he did? He diverted the flow of a river, running it straight through the Augean mess, and washing it clean in short order."

I NODDED absently. "Have you got a brainstorm?"

As it turned out, she did. "Sure. You're too wrapped up in this thing. You can't see the forest for the trees. Look, Paul, I don't know how, but you can divert the flow of a river too. What flows in a gaming room?"

"Why...money."

"Sure, and most of it flows into the coffers of the management. It's got to work that way because the tables are fixed! Oh, it's not crooked, not really... But just fixed enough to assure the house that even if every law of chance turns against it on any one night, it can't lose much. If you can divert that river of money, if you can make enough of it flow into the hands of the players, you'll force Joaquin to close down or go broke. Think about it, Paul."

She had an idea, all right. If I could get back into the gaming room before it opened, and if I could make some adjustments on the electromagnets under the roulette wheels, then—

I hardly had time to pursue my thoughts. Harold Purness *harumphed* over my shoulder and, after introducing him to Laura, I asked him to join us. He nodded, sat down, turned at once to business.

"What's on your mind, Reardon?"

"Not yet," I told him mysteriously. In truth, I hadn't considered what I'd tell the sour-faced man at all. "Listen," I said, hunching over and leaning my chin on my hands. "For now there's one thing you can do. See Joaquin over there, near the bar? All right, keep him there. Don't let him leave this room for the next fifteen minutes or so. Then, we'll see."

Purness shrugged. "Shouldn't be hard, although I don't figure your angle, Reardon. Okay," he said, getting up. "I'll keep old Joker occupied. Then you better have something mighty potent on your mind."

"Excuse me," I told Laura, rising. "I'll be back soon. With the way to win a million bucks, I hope."

THE THIRD match burned my fingers in the darkness of the gaming room before I realized there just weren't any electromagnets in the place. I swore softly to myself. I'd read a book once about roulette tables and magnetic devices that keep the game going in the house's favor. Not this house, damn it! Joaquin used some other method. So, if I were to make like Hercules by diverting the flow of a certain river, I'd have to employ another method too. Only trouble was, I didn't have any.

A crack of light opened into a wide swath for a moment, then faded away again. The door to the gaming room—which meant someone lurked within it now. Well, only Laura knew I was here.

"Laura!" I whispered. "This way, over here."

Footsteps shuffled across the floor. Laura? I acted like a prize boob. Who else could it be? And so I lit a match.

It was a mistake.

Feet running, pounding heavily on the floor, then something slamming down over my shoulders, and the match snuffed out. I fought, striking out wildly with my fists, whiffing at air mostly. The silence made the whole thing seem ridiculous. Add that to the darkness, and I could have struggled in a fantastic nightmare of my own making...

Someone clutched at my legs and I stamped back and down with my heel. Contact with something soft, a hand maybe. A muttered oath, and I stood clear, breathing heavily. I hurtled toward the door, crashing into a hard barrier of human flesh halfway there.

The man grabbed me, but I had already lost my balance and when a fist pile-drived into my solar plexus all the air whooshed out of my lungs and I tumbled over backwards.

He was very thorough. He didn't give me a chance, following me down and pounding my head like it was a much-abused punching bag. If I had any breath left to talk, I think I'd have hollered quits, but all I could do was lie there and take it. I took plenty. By the time someone turned on the lights and put an end to the carnage, my face must have looked like hamburger. If I could have saved the world just by moving my pinky, I don't think I would have been able to do it.

"So!" a voice cried. "She was right!"

"It sure looks that way. Better get her—and the boss."

I blinked, but I still couldn't see anything except a red haze. Half-conscious, I wondered idly if Diuniun somehow was watching. I sure had made a mess of things.

More lights, and something cold and wet splashing over my face. A band pushed its way under my neck and prodded. "Come on, chump. Sit up."

I made it about a third of the way, then slumped down again. More water sloshed over my face. I sat up slowly, felt myself dragged to my feet and deposited in a big chair. It felt very comfortable.

I OPENED my eyes. Phil's companion that night they almost got me with a couple of knives stood off to the left, rubbing his bruised knuckles thoughtfully. Phil himself leaned back against a dice table across the room, sitting very stiff and straight and uncomfortable, a big bandage over the bottom of his face. Angus paced back and forth nervously, muttering to himself. Hadman was smiling prettily, standing with hands on hips, drumming her fingers in an I-told-you-so way against her hipbones. Joaquin stood at the window, hands behind his back, contemplating the night.

He whirled around and stalked in my direction, angry. "Just what the hell were you trying to do, Paul?"

"You wouldn't believe me if I told you," I managed to say. My voice sounded like a couple of bullfrogs arguing with each other.

"I can tell you," Hadman said. "He thought he could somehow fix your tables and win himself a pile of money."

Joaquin asked, "Is that true?"

I said nothing, but Phil's companion started to play around in an ungentle way with my bleeding face. I shrugged. "Yes and no. Yes, I tried to fix the tables. No, I didn't give a damn if I won a penny or not."

"How could you fix it?" Joaquin seemed incredulous. "Electromagnetic contraptions went out a decade ago, Paul. It's all scientifically arranged now—without any mechanical tricks. But that's not important. I liked you, Paul; you know that. Why did you try to do it?"

"You wouldn't understand."

"Well, I'd suggest you attempt an explanation. Better grasp at straws, Paul, because you haven't got much else to grasp at."

"I say kill him," Phil mumbled thickly under his bandages. You couldn't blame him. Phil had never been a lovely creature, but that night I think I had done a good job of worsening what all the little genes and chromosomes had put together.

"Naa." This was Phil's companion of that escapade. "Not with all them soldiers in town. We'd never get away with it."

Joaquin was still angry, and ready to vent his spleen in any direction. "If you gentlemen will shut up, we can get on with this."

Maybe if I goaded him, I thought, he might switch targets altogether. I suppose I was really grasping at straws, because I had a hunch that's what my life hung on at that moment—a thin, bending straw. "Wait a minute," I told Joaquin, "I thought you said you'd get rid of these two boys after what they tried to do?"

He spread his hands out wide. "Hadman wanted them to stay. Hadman—"

"Oh. Hadman, eh?" I smiled.

JOAQUIN came close, but he did not lose his composure. He lit a cigarette, stalked to and fro for a while. By the time he turned to face me again, he inhaled slowly and let the smoke curl from his nostrils, the polished Continental again. "Now, Paul—why?"

"Remember that day I came here? Think back to it. Remember I said I thought a whole lot more than Merryville stood in the balance? It's like that. Just give me time, Joaquin, a little time. If I can't prove it to you in ten days, or if you aren't willing to forget about the whole thing, I'll surrender myself to you. I mean it." I did, too. Because in ten days we'd know one way or the other. In ten days mankind would either own the Earth again, or mankind would start packing for an Exodus that probably would spell doom for the race.

I could tell Hadman was furious, but she certainly tried not to show it. I had gotten to know her little quirks. A muscle twitched vaguely in her cheek, she brushed a lock of wine-red hair from her brow, her fingers twined tightly together. To everyone else in the room she could have been a study in indifference, but inside I knew she was boiling. "Don't listen to him, Enrico. The least you can do is throw him out and tell him to stay out." Sure, that would suit her fine, because then Labor One would go by the board as a complete failure.

I snickered. "So you kept Phil and his boyfriend on Hadman's orders, huh? Tch-tch." *Play on his pride,* I thought, *because the man has plenty.*

"I…uh…"

"And now you'd listen to her again, not even giving me a chance. Just the ten days I asked for. Who owns this place, Joaquin, you, or Hadman?"

Hadman laughed nervously. "Don't you see what he's trying to do? Work around your pride, that's what—"

"Shut up, both of you!" Joaquin stormed. "Let me think…think… Hmmm…what's the use? I stand to lose both ways… Paul, you have your ten days. You're free to do what you want. No, Hadman, don't say another word. I have spoken, and that is my decision."

"You'll probably regret it," said Hadman.

I got up, weak and dizzy, and headed for the washroom. "He won't," I told her. "Not if he's smart. But I hope to hell you will, Hadman."

CHAPTER FIVE
Of Labors Three

I TOOK TWO handfuls of paper towel out of the automatic dispensing machine in the washroom, soaking them thoroughly and bathing my face with them. I observed my work in the mirror, deciding that I didn't look too bad. A mouse showed signs of developing under my right eye and my jaw was bruised and tender on both sides.

But any way you looked at it, Hadman had me coming and going. She had read my mind; she knew what I planned—and the result came close to placing me on my back in a casket. I couldn't doubt that Diuniun was aware of her unfair advantage. The power resided in his hands and he had yielded it to her. What was it Diuniun had told me: the essence of his purple-skinned folk was fairness? Something like that, and it gave me an idea. If I could be vouchsafed the same power…

A washroom is a ridiculous place for a kind of seance, but nevertheless I found myself talking to thin air. "Diuniun, Diuniun, can you hear me?"

Nothing.

A stupid gesture and I was ready to give it up after the first try. Lord, I really wanted a miracle. How far could the little purple man's ability extend?

You're troubled, Paul Reardon. Can I help?

Mellow harp strings—a voice! Not aloud, but strumming musically inside my skull. Diuniun!

"You're damn right I'm in trouble." I proceeded to tell him.

69

I know. And there is muck to what you say. You suggest that out of fairness I should equalize things. But Reardon, if I gave you a limited form of ESP, you'd not be responding with the native abilities of your people. I question the fairness in that…

"Hell, how did Hadman get her own precognition?"

Why, I gave it to her. Yes, I did. Umm-mm. Then perhaps I could equalize the situation by withdrawing it. Yes…

The little wheels within wheels spun around madly inside my head. Ideas came fast and furious, tumbling one atop the other. No, I wouldn't want Diuniun to do that. I had a much better plan. "Why don't you give me the same power instead?" I demanded, "Hadman's used it all along, and the least you can do—"

For the first time, Diuniun sounded mildly angry. *Don't tell me what I can do. That's Hadman's trouble. But I see you mean no harm. Reardon, I grant it! Simple—precognition exists potentially in the frontal lobes of every man's brain. Just a question of applying it. In two hundred years, perhaps, your whole race… Well, no matter. You now have a limited form of ESP, Paul Reardon. Good Luck!*

That was all. A porter stood, scratching his head, in the alcove that led to the washroom. Evidently he'd eavesdropped on the one-way monologue, and now his eyes followed me as I departed. I could almost feel them piercing the back of my head.

LAURA SAT sipping another drink. Purness was looking at his wristwatch. And Quinn Berkeley had joined them, garbed in a mayor's Sunday best.

"What on earth happened to you?" aksed Laura. "You look like—"

"I tried to keep him at the bar," Purness said, "but some of his flunkies called, and he went running. I'd never have suspected Joaquin had anything to do with that coffee shop thing."

"I didn't say he had."

"Wh—what? Then why all the commotion?"

"When do I get my chance to meet Hadman?" Mayor Berkeley wanted to know.

"Paul," Laura again, "did my plan backfire, did it kick you like a mule? My gosh, I'm sorry."

"Hey, whoa! One at a time. I can't follow all of you." As a matter of fact, I could. I somehow grasped all the thoughts before they were uttered, and that supplied at least one answer. Diuniun, bless him, had come across. Precognition...

"What happens next?" Purness growled. "I broke an engagement to come here, and—"

Precognition, I realized, wouldn't do it alone. I needed Berkeley and Purness because their wallets bulged with the good green stuff which, applied expertly, might yet chalk up Labor One on Earth's side.

"Laura," I said, "your plan only backfired once. But it didn't fail without giving us a better one—same general idea. You know, that diverted river."

"What are you talking about?" Quinn Berkeley's voice boomed. "I came here because you assured me a date with Hadman. I'm here. Where's Hadman? I don't understand what's going on—"

"Nor do I," Purness joined him, irritably.

I smiled. What a motley crew of World Savers! "Listen," I said, "if you can forget temporarily, both of you, what I called you here for, how'd you like to make a killing? Enough to put you on easy street for a long time?"

"I don't need it, thanks," Purness said. "I make plenty of money...but if you say it's a sure thing—"

"You bet," I told him. "Sure thing. Mayor Berkeley?"

His Honor rubbed his hands together. "Well, a mayor's salary doesn't exactly make you a millionaire. I'm game—if I like your proposition. Let's hear it."

"We just go back to the gaming room and play some roulette," I told them blandly.

"That does it!" Purness cried, standing up. "The man's crazy. You can't beat the house at roulette, Reardon. I'm going home."

I shoved him back down in his seat. "Just a chance," I said. "All I want you to do is watch me at that roulette table. If you like what you see, you can play along. If not—okay, you beat it."

Purness sat down, grumbling. Mayor Berkeley lit a long cigar and puffed away on it thoughtfully. Laura was laughing. "Paul! Paul, you almost can convince a girl—"

I winked at her. "Just give me time, baby."

She looked doubtfully at my battered face. "If you stay in one piece long enough, Paul."

NINE-THIRTY that evening. Hadman ran offstage amidst thunderous applause. People began to drift into the gaming room.

I purchased twenty dollars' worth of chips—four blues. Laura followed me doubtfully, Quinn Berkeley and Purness with open scorn on their faces. The croupier at the roulette wheel looked like an anxious little penguin with a hyperthyroid condition, hands and eyes darting nervously, tongue licking thin lips, formal clothing all neat and stiff. "Your bets, gentlemen," he droned.

Out of nowhere, the number fourteen spun into my mind. I was nervous. Diuniun's ESP gift—or an overwrought imagination grasping at more straws? I shoved two blue chips into the square marked fourteen. Two or three other gamblers placed their bets.

The croupier spun his wheel.

It whirled swiftly, then the whirring sound slowed into a shrill tattoo of clicks. The little pellet jumped crazily from socket to socket. Jumped—

"Fourteen and red," droned the croupier, raking a pile of chips in my direction.

"Gosh!" Laura squeezed my hand.

Berkeley cleared his throat, the tip of his cigar glowing a bright red. "Luck," Purness growled under his breath.

My head pounded dully—and something whispered "eight" over and over again. I stacked ten blues carefully in the square marked with the number eight, watching the croupier activate his machine.

"Eight and red," he said, and the blue chips made a jumbled heap in front of me.

I smiled. "It all rides on twenty-three."

"All of it?" demanded the croupier, his eyes very bright.

"That's what I said."

Quinn Berkeley ran to the teller's window for chips, returning with a few hundred dollars worth. He grinned nervously, counting out a pile of chips. "A hundred dollars on twenty-three," he said.

Purness merely grunted, and the wheel spun again.

"Twenty-three and black," the croupier informed us, running a finger between his collar and his neck. Berkeley and I now had a small mountain of chips between us.

I said, "Twenty-three looks fine again. All mine ride right there."

The Mayor chuckled at some secret joke. "Me too," he declared.

Purness sent a boy running for chips, receiving them in time to put fifty dollars on twenty-three. Laura clutched my arm. "Paul, Paul—what's happening? You'll have me believing every word you said in another moment. Three straight wins. You know what the odds are against that?"

BY NOW the dice tables, the chuck-a-luck cages, the blackjack and red-dog boards—all had been deserted. Joaquin's steerers gave it up as a hopeless cause when no one could be enticed away to the other games, and the steerers also came to watch. A big half-circle formed in the glaring yellow light of the roulette table, and scores of chips cascaded down on twenty-three.

Sweating now under the hot lights, the croupier spun his wheel. His slightly ruffled. "Twenty-three and red" sounded like thunder in the silence.

People grinned, pounded one another on the back, then turned to wait for my next move. The croupier had to send for another basket of chips and, plainly, he was worried.

"Amazing!" Quinn Berkeley boomed. "Positively amazing!"

Purness said, "I take it back, Reardon. I don't know how you do it, and I don't care, as long as you can keep it up."

"It's better than a date with Hadman anytime," Berkeley admitted.

"What is?"

I whirled about. Hadman stood at my shoulder.

She wore a low-cut gown, which would make a television neckline look like a turtleneck sweater. Her perfume was not of this world, it would have caused too much trouble. Under her breath she mumbled, "That's a cheap trick, Paul."

I laughed. "You didn't mind using it, did you? With these stakes, Hadman, I'd do anything." I meant it. You don't get squeamish when the Earth hangs in the balance. I turned to the croupier. "Everything on twenty-five."

The croupier snapped his fingers, and a boy ran up to him. "Call Mr. Joaquin," the sweating man told him. "Quickly."

He fumbled with a cigarette, inserting it in a long silver holder. He took a lot of trouble with his lighter to kill time. Joaquin elbowed through the crowd before the wheel was spun. He took in the situation with a quick professional glance, looked at the croupier who muttered, "Bad, Mr. Joaquin. Very bad."

Joaquin shrugged gamely. "All right," he said. "I'll spin the wheel myself." He did.

"Twenty-five and black," he said a moment later.

I GRABBED his arm and led him, unresisting, toward a corner of the room. The crowd stirred uneasily when I left the table, and Purness tried to stop me. I shoved him away.

"Joaquin, you remember what Hadman could do with the cards? It's like that with me now. I can't lose."

He smiled. "Life is a gamble, my friend. But what under God could give you that power?"

I didn't attempt to answer. Instead, I said, "Remember, Joaquin, a lot more than Merryville will be determined by what happens here?"

"What has that to do with me?"

"Plenty. Can your man cover again if I call another number with most of the people in this room tagging along?"

"No," he admitted. "We'd go broke. Still, we can't stop. I'd be a laughing stock. I'd——"

"Damn it, Joaquin, swallow your pride! Swallow it so you can live to play again tomorrow."

"What would you have me do?"

"Close the gambling hall—for ten days. That's all I ask."

"Fantastic! I can't do that——"

He needed a way to save face, if not with his friends, at least with himself. I sensed that he was groping for one now, wondering if I had one to give him. "Listen," I tried to soothe him, "I have three—directives. One of them is this: a petulant, arbitrary thing, but there it is. Hell, I don't want your money. I just want you to close. Joaquin, you, everybody, the whole human race would want me to win. Three directives, and this is the first. Do you close?"

He mused, half to himself, about Hadman, about Merryville's losing fight with improbabilities, about the power to forsee. He said, "By God, Paul, if you're lying—"

"I'm not. Shut down and we can all go home happy. Round one will be over."

He didn't answer, and I thought for a moment I had lost. He ran a hand through his sleek black hair, arranged his bow tie carefully, and flicked a speck of lint off the shoulder of his tuxedo. He walked slowly, as in a daze, to the far end of the room, past the idle rows of chuck-a-luck cages, past the dice waiting patiently on their green cushions, past the neatly stacked cards on the blackjack tables.

He reached the far wall, still in deep thought, and he banged on the wall for silence. Heads lifted from their concentration on the roulette table, and soon everyone in the hall had turned to face him.

"My friends," Joaquin said slowly, "I won't attempt to explain. Sometimes a man of headstrong pride, a man such as you know your friend Joaquin to be, can be struck—struck just once in his lifetime—by whatever mysterious thing there is that makes people humble. Thus, it is not due to any reverses we may have suffered, and it is not because of anything I can tell you, but the gaming room will be closed for the next ten days.

"Wait." He held up his hands for silence. "Life goes on elsewhere in Twin Oaks. All drinks tonight are on the house, and Hadman will dance as she never has danced before. Now please cash in your chips."

LAURA WAS a little tight as we took a taxi home. "What did you do with all the money you won, Paul?"

"I gave it back to Joaquin," I told her. "The poor guy can use it."

"You—what? Paul, you positively intriguing idiot—I believe you! Yes, I believe everything you told me. Ooo...Paul..."

She slumped over toward me, her head lolling on my shoulder. "Paul, I feel so giddy—"

I cupped her cheeks in my hands and kissed her. It seemed the natural thing to do. No wild, impossible other-worldly passion in that kiss, not the kind that Hadman offered with her lips. But Laura did not respond with a sisterly peck. She clung to me fiercely, and I heard the driver snickering as we went at it. Laura could hold her own with the girls of Earth, and that was enough.

It was then that the cab stopped with a screeching of brakes and a whining protest from its tires. A big gray sedan had forced us off the road and onto its shoulder.

The cabby flung his door open and hopped out, a big clumsy man. "What the hell is this?" he demanded. Then: "Cripes, a gun! Okay, boys—I'm sorry. I don't care what the hell it is. Just lemme alone."

Phil's bandaged face peered into the back window. "Come on out, you two."

We got out of the cab and into the sedan. Phil climbed into the back seat beside us, holding a snub-nosed .45 idly in his hand. "No tricks," he warned.

In the darkness, his companion struck heavily at the cab driver's head, with a gun probably. The cabbie moaned once, then fell on his face.

The road to Twin Oaks winds its way outside of Merryville, but the army had decided to include Joaquin's establishment as part of the city limits, and only routine questioning faced us at the beginning of Main Street. Phil kept us very quiet in the back seat, and when the driver responded to his interrogators, I recognized Angus' voice!

WE DROVE in silence down into the slums which border on the railroad tracks, and Angus pulled the car smoothly into an ancient weather-beaten garage.

"Out," Phil barked. "Don't tempt me, Reardon, 'cause I'd love to knock you off. Just give me a lead."

He wasn't kidding. If he lived to be a hundred, he wouldn't forget that night I kicked his teeth in.

Angus seemed apologetic, but then Angus had changed. He spoke almost in a whine, his eyes casting anxious, furtive glances in all directions. He was, I realized, wound hopelessly around Hadman's little finger.

The house adjacent to the garage was an old clapboard affair. Shingles, which had fallen from the roof, lay untouched on the sparse lawn. The gate squeaked when Phil opened it, and his key found the going difficult with the tumblers in the door lock.

"Hurry up," Angus told him. "She said to hurry."

"Keep your shirt on, Scotty. She'll keep another minute."

We climbed a flight of stairs, dimly lit by a dirty glazed bulb on the landing. Phil ushered us into a large living room on the second floor, shoving us forward unnecessarily. Laura stumbled and fell, moaning, and I wheeled about, ready to jump at the gunman.

He waved his .45 in my face. "I wouldn't advise it, chum. But cripes, it's your life. Go ahead."

"Stop it," Hadman said. She came to us from the far end of the living room. Not a flicker of emotion crossed her features, but she slapped Phil smartly across the face. "I didn't say anything about getting rough, did I? Why don't you follow instructions, like Angus?"

Angus liked that. He beamed. I almost thought he'd sound off like a contented lap dog. And the web had been woven at least partially about Phil. He took the blow stolidly, even mumbling he was sorry.

I tried to read Hadman's mind with the powers Diuniun had given me—and got a blank!

"Don't try so hard," she said. "Diuniun stripped you of your ESP. He knew what you wanted it for, let you use it for that. But it ends right here."

SO I WAS on my own. With two labors to go. But hell, I couldn't even get started, couldn't even find out what they were, not with Phil's gun staring down my throat. I asked Hadman, "Why'd you bring us here?"

"Don't tell me you don't know! You won on your first task, Paul. That's enough. Old Diuniun might get bitter if I had you killed outright, so I decided to detain you instead. Ten days, that's not a very long time. Ten days—and then the Earth is mine! Could you realize what it would be like for my people, living like a bunch of Spartans off on the other end of the Galaxy, to find a green Earth waiting for them? Oh, Diuniun and his crowd don't much care. They're versatile; they can adapt to almost any environment. But my people, we were born for Earth just as you were."

"Nuts," I told her. "Diuniun let me in on that. You grew spoiled out there in space. You don't deserve anything, let alone this planet."

Hadman's laughter was mocking. "Well, we're going to get it, with the Overlords. You know, Paul, of all the men of Earth, you alone I could have liked. Could have—well, no matter. You brought all this on yourself..."

Angus did not understand much of the conversation, but he hated those last words. He still looked like a puppy, but not a lapdog. Rather, a beaten cur now, sulking off in a corner. Hadman must have noticed. She called, softly, "Come here, Angus."

He came to her, licking his internal wounds. She stroked him! Yes, stroked him—running her hand slowly along the nape of his neck, along his shoulders, his arm—exactly the way you might pet an animal. Angus smiled quite contentedly when she finished, and Phil scratched his head.

"What a bunch o' loons!" he said. "I dunno—"

"Well, this much you know," Hadman told him. "Paul and this girl here—" Laura had slumped down dejectedly in a chair, very tired, and more than a little high—"Paul and this girl will use that room down the hall. You guard it, Phil, alternating with Angus. They are not to leave. Is that understood?"

"Sure," Phil smiled cheerfully. This was something he could comprehend, and he liked the idea. He'd even like it better if we tried to escape, because then he'd have a good excuse to ventilate me with his .45. It's a big gun and it makes big holes. I could just see Phil smiling out from behind the acrid smoke with his bandaged face. But if it came to that, I wouldn't see anything at all.

We were dog-tired, Laura and I, by the time Phil pushed us ahead of him into the room, then went out, closing and locking the door behind him. Laura threw herself across the bed, sobbing a little. Then she stopped. She sat up, smiling through her tears.

"Scared, kid?" I asked her. I had crossed the room to its one window, found that it was barred—a new job and a quick one, because the plaster still was fresh and a lot of it had caked loosely around the sill.

"I—I guess so," Laura admitted. "But not anymore, Paul. Gee, I was crying just like a baby, wasn't I? Well, it won't happen again. And whatever does happen, I believe you. And the whole thing still intrigues me."

IT INTRIGUED her! Guarded by a trigger-happy gunman and she was intrigued. I grunted something about that under my breath, but then I smiled. In spite of this mess, I found myself liking Laura more and more every moment.

"I can't help it," Laura told me, smiling now. "I guess I always liked to see new and different things because—"

"I know. They intrigue you!" I laughed, then stretched myself out on the floor.

"Don't tell me you're going to sleep there!"

"Where else?" The room had a chest-of-drawers, two straight-backed chairs, and the one big over-sized bed.

Laura patted the other side of the bed. "Why, right here, of course."

"Huh?"

"My gosh, Paul. I can trust you."

Well, that's the way Laura is. And I wouldn't have believed it myself. I got up and lay on one side of the bed, near the edge. Laura isn't very big, and she lay on the other side. There was a lot of room between us, and it stayed that way all night. What's the word, platonic? I didn't even kiss her goodnight. Maybe I didn't trust myself. But Laura did. She was breathing easily in a couple of minutes.

And she had a good-morning kiss for me, which made everything seem worth our trouble. I don't go around probing into my emotions, because that has a way of spoiling them. But in the morning I knew I was falling in love with Laura.

What did it matter? I could hear Angus or Phil walking around outside. It looked a hell of a lot like mankind was doomed.

THE DAYS swept by alarmingly fast. Twice daily, Phil brought us food, making snide remarks about the closeness of our relationship in the little room. We heard muted evidence of a lot of activity on the ground floor. By day, a whole battery of workmen would arrive, clattering around with their tools and lumber, converting the dilapidated old house, I reasoned, into a sort of mansion for Hadman, who by this time scoffed at hotel rooms and their transient nature.

Several times we tried to attract their attention. I stamped on the floor and beat at the door with my fists. Laura yelled until her throat was sore. But downstairs the tools clattered merrily away and I told Laura once—ruefully—that it was like spitting against the wind.

On Wednesday of the following week, Phil didn't think so. He barged into our room without warning, and I felt like a kid caught with his fist in the cookie jar. Phil had a sense of humor. Quite innocently, he thanked me for the opportunity, then slashed down with the butt of his pistol across my forehead.

Just like that. No preambles. I remember staggering back across the bed, remember Phil whistling as he stalked from the room. Then my head was pillowed in Laura's lap. She had wet a towel in the bathroom that adjoins our quarters and the water sloshed down across my face as she soothed my forehead with it. "Feel better, honey?"

I grinned. "I guess it didn't work, kid. You know what today is? Wednesday. The seventh day. Three more to go, and then we lose. What the hell, even if we got out today, we wouldn't have time to play around with Diuniun's next two labors."

Laura wrung the towel out over my face and I got up spluttering. "Hey—cut it out!"

"Cut it out nothing! Don't talk like that, that's all. We don't lose until your little purple friend carts us off someplace like the Pied Piper. And don't you forget it."

I didn't. There was more optimism in Laura with her chestnut hair and pert little face than in a hall full of sweepstakes ticket holders. Unfortunately, mere optimism wouldn't be enough, not with the deadline for Diuniun's decision coming on Saturday.

The activity in Hadman's rapidly blossoming mansion did not abate in the early morning hours. Each evening she'd go to Twin Oaks for her two appearances, and she'd never return alone. Often we heard voices downstairs, most of which we failed to recognize. But there was a lot of gaiety and a lot of laughter, and three times at least we thought we heard Quinn Berkeley's booming accents.

ON THURSDAY morning I got a message from Diuniun. I don't know how he posted his last letter, and he certainly couldn't post one to me this time. Instead, he talked inside my head, like that time at the washroom séance. It came as a faint buzzing first, the kind you hear when you pick up a seashell and hold it, near your ear. I must have stood like a devotee at some invisible shrine, because Laura looked at me queerly. I held a finger to my lips for silence, and she didn't argue. By this time she was willing to accept anything.

The buzzing melted into the harp-tones of Diuniun's voice! *Hercules had his animals to tame—the Nemean Lion, the Hydra, others. There are in Merryville men who are Hadman's animals. These you are to tame in one way or another: Angus McDougle, Joaquin, Mayor Berkeley. The time grows short, Reardon..."*

"What happened?" Laura said. "Diuniun spoke. Yeah, stop looking at me like that. Okay?"

"O-okay, I guess. You don't mind if I'm a little doubtful?"

I shrugged. "Two things about his message stink to high heaven. First, he must know we're trapped here, but he didn't say a thing about it. He—"

"He's not going to do our work for us, that's all. You told me he said you'd have to win through on your own merits."

"All right. I'll grant that. But he said Quinn Berkeley was one of Hadman's cronies."

'So what? We'll have to believe him, Paul. We heard Berkeley here a few times, remember? I only saw your gal Hadman a couple of times, and not too closely. But she has sex appeal with the biggest capital S ever written. Berkeley would be a natural for her. Boy, what I wouldn't do with that figure…"

I looked Laura up and down severely, and after a while she got alarmed. "Hey, what are you trying to do?"

"I'm just making comparisons," I laughed. "Laura, you don't have to take a back seat, not for my money. When we get out of here—"

Then she was cuddling in my arms, and she fit there. "Paul, do you think we'll ever get out? I mean alive? I mean, in time? Paul—"

Well, that was Laura. She had dropped her optimism in my lap, and it left her afraid.

CAME FRIDAY night, we both were afraid. Downstairs, Quinn Berkeley's voice shook the walls. Once or twice we heard another man talking, possibly Joaquin. I fingered the swollen cut on my forehead, and Laura said: "Do you really want to try again?"

I patted her hand, kissed her lightly on the cheek. "Listen, don't you do an about-face. Of course we're going to try.

Only this time we're going to make so much noise that the whole neighborhood comes running."

I lifted one of the straight-backed chairs over my head and brought it down with a crash on the floor, selecting a man-sized club out of the debris. I commenced beating a war-chant with it, and I didn't stop for breath.

Laura cried "Help!" over and over again, at the top of her voice. It can be a very effective word. It's sure to bring results, time-tests like all those products you hear about via the radio. Only sometimes the nature of the results are a problem. We heard a key slipping into the lock and heard the tumblers fall. Phil poked his angry face inside the door, this time minus the bandages. His jaw looked a little crooked. His gun didn't.

"Son," he gritted, "you're gonna wish you went to sleep early tonight."

He came for me, the .45 gripped in his hand like a club.

My club was bigger.

I hid it behind my back until Phil's face leered not a yard from me, until he lifted the gun over his head and started it on its downward arc. Then I struck, and it sounded just like a big stick breaking when the chair-leg bounced off Phil's jaw—his newly healed, if crooked, jaw. There wasn't a scratch on the chair leg.

I think that as he fell Phil knew his jaw had fractured again, because his scream was as much one of indignation as of pain. A nasty break this time, with a jagged chunk of bone protruding out of the lacerated skin below his lips.

Laura turned away and I tossed her the .45. "I kind of favor this club," I told her, hefting it in my hands.

She looked at me. "Don't act melodramatic!"

"I'm not. If I ran downstairs with that gun, I'd be liable to shoot up everything in sight." I guess I was plenty mad. Phil deserved all he got, but that wasn't it. Angus and Joaquin played Hadman's game, and Earth hung in the balance. Angus I couldn't lay any blame—he didn't know what was going on. But Joaquin knew at least the half of it, and Quinn Berkeley, well, we'd have to see about His Honor.

As we ran down the stairs I called over my shoulder, "You know how to use that thing? You squeeze the trigger and brace yourself so the recoil doesn't knock you through the wall."

THEY SAT in the parlor, its walls freshly papered, playing bridge. That's what I said, with the fate of the world dangling before their eyes, they played bridge!

"...this is slaughter," Joaquin was saying. "You can read those cards even before they're played, Hadman."

"I doubt it," Major Berkeley assured him. Some men never learn. "It's just incredible luck my partner's got, like that time what's-his-name—Reardon?—like that time he had a run at roulette. Of course, if you and McDougle here want to quit—"

Of them all, Angus was the most anxious. "What's keeping Phil so long? You'd think he'd be down by now."

Hadman smiled. "Don't worry. The way he feels about our friend upstairs, Phil can take care of himself."

"Who is upstairs, anyway?" Joaquin demanded, putting his cards down. "Who's been making all that noise?"

"Ah! This was Hadman. "Hear him? He's coming downstairs now. What say, Enrico? Who's up there? Why, no one important. Don't let it disturb you. Don't—"

"I was upstairs," I said.

Laura wouldn't be outdone. "Me too."

Angus got up fast, starting toward us, but he stared at the gun in Laura's hand, and he sat down again.

"Reardon!" Mayor Berkeley boomed. "This is an unexpected pleasure. Whatever happened after you won all that money at Twin Oaks? Lord, will you tell that young woman to put that thing down?"

Hadman seemed unruffled. "I too heard Diuniun's second message, Paul. Just what do you think you're going to do, kill us all?"

"Kill us!" cried Quinn Berkeley. "Hah-hah, you're joking. Hadman, how you can joke! You—are joking? Hadman? Why should Reardon want to kill us? Reardon," he blubbered, "please tell me she's joking!"

"You see," Hadman observed coolly, "they don't even know what's happening. You can't destroy them, Paul, because there are certain laws here which would carry the game through to its logical conclusion, destroying you as well. And the girl, such a pretty little thing. Would you want her destroyed?"

"Go to hell," I said. "You don't talk your way out of anything this time," I crossed the room to a large bay window, half-hidden behind elaborate drapery. "We don't have to kill them, just detain them till tomorrow night." Joaquin sighed when I ripped down the drapes.

I TORE THEM into a dozen thick strips, twisting these to give them strength, then I said: "Laura, you stand right there. If anyone moves, don't ask questions, just shoot. I'm going to tie them—"

My mistake was starting with Quinn Berkeley. Hadman had planted the idea of impending death in his head, and it stuck there. He was sweating profusely as I approached, probably thinking that I'd garrot him with the drapery. Had I trussed one of the others up first it might have been different. But Berkeley quaked like a cornered animal and, like a cornered animal, he was possessed of desperate cunning.

From him of all people I didn't expect trouble. I ordered him to clasp his hands over his head, and he brought them up to obey. They failed to stay there. I crouched in close to wrap a coil of the torn drapery around them, and they swung down from above, clubbing the back of my neck like a sledgehammer. I fell heavily across Berkeley's knees, momentarily stunned, and he tugged at a fistful of my hair with each hand.

His voice rumbled up out of a deep well, and vaguely I heard him cry, "Grab him, somebody! I can't hold on forever. Obviously, he's crazy."

Angus had another idea. He dove for Laura, jarring her knees with his shoulder. They hit the floor in a heap, rolling over and over, and then I pulled clear of Berkeley, lumbering to my feet and weaving around the room groggily. I picked up my club and stumbled toward their whirling, twisting bodies, but I was too late.

Laura lay in a sobbing, huddled heap and Angus sat near her, panting. He waved the .45 at me. "Get the hell back, Paul, or I'll kill you."

He wasn't kidding.

"I'LL CALL the police," Quinn Berkeley suggested, crossing the room toward the telephone table. "We'll have these lunatics locked up."

Hadman barred his way. "You'll do nothing of the sort. Sit down."

"What? Why shouldn't I call them? Why—"

Hadman said nothing. She twined her arms around Berkeley's neck and cooed at him. "You're so strong and— won't you do that for me?"

Quinn Berkeley was at Angus' I-like-to-be-pampered stage. But he didn't stay there long. There was something of confusion in his beady eyes, and something of fear. He pulled his big bulk away from Hadman, and she seemed so surprised that she didn't try to stop him. The Mayor said, mumbling half to himself, "No, it isn't right. I don't know what, I don't know why, but I fear you're acting outside the law here. I really fear it. No, keep away. I wanted you, Hadman. I—I still do. But all my life I rubbed my nose in the gutter to become mayor. Yes, in the gutter. And I won't jeopardize that. I'm through with you, Hadman."

He turned and started to walk away from her slowly... She shrugged. "It's just as well. We'll separate the sheep from the wolves here and now. What about you, Angus?"

He came to her quickly, and she let him hold her hand. He was content.

Joaquin scratched his head. Laura and I stood still, because although he was busy, Angus' gun-hand still pointed in our direction. Quinn Berkeley sat on the sofa, his chin resting on his hands.

I shuddered, thinking what a whole race of Hadmans, male and female, could do to our world. Oh, Diuniun and his fellows would be there too, but I suspected they'd remain aloof, relegating the task of evacuation to Hadman's gang. A word, a glance, a gesture—and they'd have the evacuees streaming into Diuniun's ships like a horde of lemmings.

I said to Joaquin, "Remember, a lot more than Merryville is at stake. There are millions of Hadmans, waiting to come here, waiting to weave their magic, waiting to take over our world. Could you see us resisting when that happens?"

"She's not of this world, then? Would you say that?" cried Joaquin.

I nodded.

"Then if she can do that to men," he gestured at Angus, "she is a spawn of the Devil. Surely not of God, Paul, because He would not permit such things." Joaquin sighed. "I longed to take her to couch with me. Hadman would play there like no woman ever did. Still, too long have I seen this strife from her camp. And now, like an ugly boil, I believe the strife is coming to a head. Perhaps I should see it from your camp, Paul, before I behave like that." He looked with contempt at Angus and spat on the floor, ranging himself beside Laura and me.

Hadman didn't even look at him. She took the .45 from Angus' nerveless fingers. "Angus," she said, "you will take the girl outside and wait in the car."

For a moment I stood between them, but Hadman waved me away irritably with her gun, and I watched helplessly as Angus led Laura, dazed and unresisting, through the door. Hadman turned to me. "I happen to know what Diuniun's next command will be, Paul. You'll never make it. You won't even come close." She wheeled about, opening the door and going out after Angus, her hips still swaying seductively. She had that to the last. I guess it was a part of her.

This time I didn't bat an eyelash when Diuniun's voice plucked its harp-strings inside my head. *Hercules had his Queen of the Amazons, Reardon, and you have your Hadman. Bring her to me.* And that was all.

I heard Hadman's car roar away from the curb outside.

CHAPTER SIX
The Final Magic

I SHOOK Quinn Berkeley's shoulder. "Better call your cops now. There's an injured man upstairs. And give me the keys to your car, quick!"

Dumbly, he fumbled in his pocket, then held the keys out for me.

With Joaquin sitting beside me, I kicked over the engine of Berkeley's Oldsmobile just as the taillights of Hadman's car disappeared around a corner two blocks away. It was a hell of a time to think of Laura, but right then she was as important to me as the fate of the world.

Both would need an awful lot of saving.

We got a flat tire a street or two this side of the military barrier at the end of Main Street. I can't be sure, but I don't think it was an accident. More of Hadman's magic, and actually it didn't seem like much in the light of what she'd done in Merryville.

I cursed impotently, pulled the Olds to a stop and hurtled out of it. Joaquin was right behind me when we reached an M.P. lounging idly against the barricade. "What's the trouble, friends?"

"Did you pass a car through here a minute ago?"

"Sure. Going out along the road to Twin Oaks. Ain't no law against it."

I had no time to explain. Instead, I brought a haymaker up from the ground and let him have it flush on the mouth. He sighed, slumping against the fence and coming to rest in an inert heap at my feet.

A jeep was parked on the other side of the barricade with two officers sitting in it studying a map. I grabbed the fallen M.P.'s rifle and vaulted over the fence. Silent as a ghost, Joaquin followed.

I barked at the two officers: "Climb out of there."

"Eh? What's that?"

I poked the major's belly with my bayonet. "I said, get out. I'm not kidding. Come on...scat! And leave the keys in the ignition."

"It's a federal offense—"

"Let me worry about that," I told them as I prodded them away from the jeep.

Then we were off, bumping and bouncing along the road to Twin Oaks. Joaquin said, "Do you see them?"

I shook my head. "No. We wasted too much time with those soldiers."

"Do you know where you're going?"

"N—no," I admitted. "You think Hadman would have any unfinished business at Twin Oaks?"

Joaquin told me he doubted it. But he thought it was as good a place as any. The plain fact stared us in the face: we didn't know what to do. Four A.M. Saturday morning, with Diuniun's decision coming at midnight. With Laura in Hadman's clutches...

WE SAT AT the deserted bar, drinking beer. There wasn't a thing we could do. I stared at Joaquin. Joaquin stared at me, and then the gambler laughed.

"It is funny," he said. "The military will be here soon, looking for their jeep. And all we can do is sit and get morose because we don't know where to find Hadman. Paul, can't you think of something—some clue that might lead us to her?"

I drank the beer in great gulps, popping the caps off new bottles almost as fast as Joaquin could get them from the icebox. "Hell, no," I told him. "I don't know a thing that—wait a minute! Yeah, wait! Come on—" I tugged at his arm, toppling his glass and spilling its contents all over the floor.

"Where to?"

We gunned the jeep back along the road to Merryville just as the sun started to climb over the low hills to the East. "I just remembered something," I cried over the shrieking wind, which a jeep meets bounding along a bumpy road at seventy miles an hour. "That day Hadman met me in her convertible, that day I was whisked away upstairs, somehow Hadman followed in a few minutes, saying something about a scout plane. It just took a few minutes, so it must have been nearby. Yes—and here's where she met me."

I stopped the jeep and we climbed out. "So what would have prevented her from taking off before this?" Joaquin demanded.

It was a good question, but Hadman supplied the answer.

A shower of stones cascaded down upon us. No source. They just came out of a spot in the sky, pelting the jeep. Joaquin tucked his head in under folded arms and cried, "What's happening?"

I shrugged. It meant Hadman was still here, and nearby. What was it she said about natural laws, they all added up to a lot of hogwash, unwarranted intuitive assumptions or some such thing? So she could hurl stones at us out of the sky and, actually, inexplicable rains of stones are more common than you might think. I'd seen an article in a Sunday supplement once, I'd—a couple of big rocks pelting uncomfortably close broke my revelry!

The important fact remained: something had detained Hadman. She had not yet left the Earth, and now that we approached, she set up her defenses.

OFF TO THE left of where we had parked the jeep, a wooded glen marched its silent trees right up to the roadside. It could begin there.

We plunged in, and I beat a path for us with the rifle.

No more stones, the trees would stop them. But Hadman would have something else waiting; she wouldn't give it up as a poor job just like that. We found out soon enough, because when I turned to see if Joaquin was following, I had to pull him down out of the foliage by his ankles. Hadman's anti-gravity trick again, only this time it wasn't funny.

Joaquin yelped, then floated away again. And abruptly, I felt incredibly light. I tried to keep my footing, but it was like attempting to remain on the bottom of the Great Salt Lake. It couldn't be done, and I floated up to join Joaquin.

"My God," he mumbled. Then, over and over, "My God."

Experimentally, I grasped a branch and, using it as a fulcrum, swung myself along. "Like a monkey." I panted. "Swing along like an ape, Enrico. It's the only way."

We swung and we made progress, and Hadman must have known. Weight returned without warning, and we plummeted to the ground, the lower branches breaking our fall. Joaquin hobbled after me. "My ankle," he muttered. "I hurt my ankle. Not me, no! That witch hurt it."

Then it began to rain. From a scientific standpoint, that was the least of Hadman's miracles, because with her defiance of the laws that science holds as sacred she had brought the militia to Merryville, while we of Earth are coming pretty close to controlling rainstorms right now by seeding the clouds with carbon dioxide.

But Hadman needed no elaborate seeding process. It merely rained—great driving sheets of rain pouring down on us, drenching the rich foliage, turning the ground into a sponge, which sucked at our ankles, beating our clothing into a sodden ruin, half-blinding us. Spears of lightning stalked us in Hadman's grim game, and once a huge tree not a dozen feet away was rent asunder by a vivid flash.

"It's fantastic!" Joaquin roared over the storm. "Impossible!"

"No. No, it's not. Call it super-science, Enrico, used ruthlessly. Call it—hell, what's the difference?"

Something gleamed close at hand, something big and sleek. Two things really, one small, the other large.

The first was Hadman's automobile, brought in through a clearing on the other side of the woods. The second—an elongated teardrop, half a hundred feet from nose to tail, metallic, glistening—Hadman's scout ship!

Acrid fumes made us cough, made our eyes tear. Hell-fires flashed and roared at the tail of the ship, belching out in tempo with a booming noise that struck outrageously at our eardrums. Meaninglessly, I raised the rifle to my shoulder and fired. The bullet ricocheted off the ship's hull with a metallic pang.

"Why don't you throw pebbles?" Joaquin scoffed as he hobbled after me.

We worked our way around to the nose of the ship. Momentarily I expected some more of Hadman's magic, but when none came I realized that perhaps the sphere of influence for such things was not so local that it would fail to snare Hadman as well. I smiled grimly. She'd have to meet us at our own terms.

A PORT yawned invitingly on the other side of the ship, and I pulled Joaquin back among the trees. "Wait," I said, "it might be a trap."

"So what? If we just stand here, she'll take off. The backlash from those jets will probably kill us anyway," It was a good point.

At that moment, angry voices floated out from the port— first Angus, then Hadman, shouting. Silence.

I almost jumped out of my shoes when a shot reverberated dully, and then someone came staggering out of the port. Angus. He walked three or four steps, erratically. He fell on his back. The front of his shirt where his hands clutched feebly was all red.

"She—wouldn't—take me," he moaned. "She was— playing with me. She—didn't want—me." He sobbed, and red flecked his lips. The last thing he uttered was, "I'll never see...Hadman again!"

I checked a wild impulse to fire a volley into the port. Laura was in there somewhere...

Joaquin ran forward, stumbling crookedly on his bad ankle, crossing Angus' corpse without looking at it. I tried to call him back, I screamed for him to stop. He'd run to his slaughter...

He didn't hear, and briefly I saw Hadman silhouetted in the port, the smoking .45 in her hand. She fired—once, twice, again.

Joaquin's body jerked convulsively with each impact, but he lumbered forward. "Witch," he was crying. "Witch, witch, witch. That's what you are."

The port started to slide shut as Joaquin reached it. He pitched forward, broken and bloody, falling into the breech, blocking it with his body.

I darted toward the ship, twisting, turning, spinning in the face of Hadman's fire. Something whizzed by my cheek. Something else burned fiercely in my shoulder, throwing me up and back like a giant hand. Then, no more shooting. Hadman crouched, pushing at Joaquin, trying to clear him from the port, sobbing now. Sobbing, for the first time, because Joaquin was wedged there, and I staggered toward them, holding the rifle in my hands but forgetting about it.

My left arm was numb, my shirt wet with a growing stain of red. Joaquin still lived. Lived a moment more! He said softly through the rain, "I died nobly, didn't I, Paul? What did my life of vice matter? What did it matter, if once, at the last moment I struck a blow for God?"

I stepped over him as he died, and Hadman—her composure an old cloak that she had discarded—hurled the empty .45 at me, screaming. It struck my injured shoulder, sent lances of pain coursing through the arm, which a moment before had felt, nothing. I dropped the rifle and reached out with my good hand, entwining it in Hadman's wine-red hair and pulling her face so close that I could have rubbed noses with her.

"You'll take this ship to Diuniun now," I said. "If you don't, I'll kill you."

Hadman looked at me, a quick darting glance that plunged deep inside my brain and read my mind. She moved listlessly toward the controls as I retrieved my rifle.

Laura was bound tightly to a stanchion, smiling serenely. "We had engine trouble and we couldn't take off for a time," she said, laughing hysterically.

* * *

DIUNIUN'S purple face stared at me soberly. "You win, Paul Reardon, and I am glad. You may take the congratulations of a tired, petulant Overlord back to your Earth with you. We'll return to our far home across the Galaxy, where we have learned to live—"

"Where?" I said. "What star?"

Little purple shoulders shrugged. "You haven't named it. Your largest telescopes haven't discovered it. But someday perhaps your progeny will come out and visit with us, eh?"

"Where's Hadman?" Laura wanted to know.

For answer, Diuniun pointed to the viewport. Briefly, something flashed away from the spaceship, not toward the shining globe of Earth, but away from it, into the bleak darkness of space.

"Hadman?" I asked.

"Hadman. She coveted too much, far too much for either human or Overlord. She lost. She could not be humble again, so she took her ship on one last flight. You would not know it, Reardon, but there is a vast, chaotic, wild freedom out there. Hadman has fuel for perhaps a hundred million miles. She wants all space as her casket."

"No," I told him. "You're wrong. Look now." The tiny midget of a scoutship turned once and then passed over us, rocketing in toward the great, fiery orb that was the sun. Diuniun was right and he was wrong. Hadman had lost and she could face it only in, death, But she didn't want interstellar space for a casket, she wanted the sun for a funeral pyre.

"About your wound," Diuniun was saying, "Come with me," I felt weak and my arm was stiff, but it had stopped bleeding. He led me to a high-vaulted room with bank upon bank of machinery standing against its walls in orderly rows. He eased me down on a low pallet, passed something over my face. I grew sleepy…

When I awoke, my arm was sound. A white scar alone remained where the bullet had done its damage, a scar that looked half a dozen years old. Impossible science of the Overlords. Yes, someday we would reach out to them, out to the stars, to share their wisdom. But we weren't yet ready.

"Potentially," Diuniun said, "you have a good world, Reardon. There is a lot of ugliness; there is corruption where a false ideology holds half Earth's people in thralldom. But it will pass. I, Diuniun, say it will pass, if your people can fight it wisely.

"Now," he grinned, "take your woman and go." From someplace off in a far corner of the room, the black cloud pulsed toward us, engulfed us, became a polished globe. I heard Diuniun's voice, from far away. "Don't forget, I gave you an extra ten days. The sun will dip back in its path, the ten days will be forgotten by Earth, Reardon. Everyone will forget. Only you will remember the month that had forty days..."

The globe took us to Earth, dissolved, became the black cloud, became nothing...

WE STOOD on Main Street in Merryville. Laura seemed very surprised to see me. "I—I know you," she said. "You're Paul Reardon." She smiled. "Are you still sticking to that wild story, Hercules?"

I smiled back at her. "No," I said. "Forget it. You're right. It was just a line, but now that you've nibbled, I can throw it away. You know what we're going to do, Laura?"

"What?"

"We're, going to paint this town red. And then you know what?"

"What?"

"We're going to fall in love."

She started to laugh. "My gosh, you're funny," She tucked her arm in under mine as I hailed a cab.

"Want to bet?" I asked her.

THE END

If you've enjoyed this book, you will not want to miss these terrific titles…

ARMCHAIR SCI-FI & HORROR DOUBLE NOVELS, $12.95 each

D-91 **THE TIME TRAP** by Henry Kuttner
THE LUNAR LICHEN by Hal Clement

D-92 **SARGASSO OF LOST STARSHIPS** by Poul Anderson
THE ICE QUEEN by Don Wilcox

D-93 **THE PRINCE OF SPACE** by Jack Williamson
POWER by Harl Vincent

D-94 **PLANET OF NO RETURN** by Howard Browne
THE ANNIHILATOR COMES by Ed Earl Repp

D-95 **THE SINISTER INVASION** by Edmond Hamilton
OPERATION TERROR by Murray Leinster

D-96 **TRANSIENT** by Ward Moore
THE WORLD-MOVER by George O. Smith

D-97 **FORTY DAYS HAS SEPTEMBER** by Milton Lesser
THE DEVIL'S PLANET by David Wright O'Brien

D-98 **THE CYBERENE** by Rog Phillips
BADGE OF INFAMY by Lester del Rey

D-99 **THE JUSTICE OF MARTIN BRAND** by Raymond A. Palmer
BRING BACK MY BRAIN by Dwight V. Swain

D-100 **WIDE-OPEN PLANET** by L. Sprague de Camp
AND THEN THE TOWN TOOK OFF by Richard Wilson

ARMCHAIR SCIENCE FICTION CLASSICS, $12.95 each

C-31 **THE GOLDEN GUARDSMEN**
by S. J. Byrne

C-32 **ONE AGAINST THE MOON**
by Donald A. Wollheim

C-33 **HIDDEN CITY**
by Chester S. Geier

ARMCHAIR SCIENCE FICTION & HORROR GEMS SERIES, $12.95 each

G-9 **SCIENCE FICTION GEMS, Vol. Five**
Clifford D. Simak and others

G-10 **HORROR GEMS, Vol. Five**
E. Hoffman Price and others

COLD, CALCULATED ATTACK FROM SPACE

Cardigan and Bennett had developed a helluva business. It was a lucrative mining operation for vardium on the distant planet of Igakuro. And the Federation always bought everything they brought up out of the ground—at high prices, too. Little did they suspect, though, that they were being targeted by a band of interplanetary pirates. The pirates' leader, a merciless outer space thug named Satan, had plans of taking over their entire operation—and he didn't mind using an atomic pistol and taking a few lives in doing it. Making things even more complicated was the arrival of a space missionary and his beautiful daughter on the eve of the pirates' attack! They soon found out what hell was really all about…

David Wright O'Brien was one of the best writers in Ray Palmer's stable of writers for Amazing Stories *and* Fantastic Adventures *in the early 1940s. His work is largely forgotten, but there's no doubt that Wright (the nephew of* Weird Tales *founder Farnsworth Wright) knew how to spin wildly entertaining yarns. He died in 1944 at age 26 in a bombing raid over Berlin. "The Devil's Planet" is a grand outer space adventure tale and a fine example of his story-telling prowess.*

CAST OF CHARACTERS

CLEVE CARDIGAN
He was a hardheaded partner in a lucrative mining operation on a faraway planet—and he sure as hell didn't like visitors.

PETE BENNETT
Cardigan's partner, the reasonable one. He didn't mind outer space visitors, especially if they were blonde and good-looking.

REVEREND ZENDER
On the surface he seemed like a typical old-fashioned, stalwart space missionary. Looks can be deceiving, though.

SATAN
This notorious space marauder wasn't afraid of anyone, anything, or even of pulling a trigger on one of his own men.

CAROL ZENDER
Pete Bennett was swept away by her striking beauty and her charm. She was much more than a pretty face, though.

CAP HUTCH
This crotchety old space tramp was a good man at heart, but his stop on Igakuro brought him far more than he bargained for.

TORGAN
Crude and uneducated—yet his native abilities were crucially important in the fight against invading space marauders.

THE DEVIL'S PLANET

By
DAVID WRIGHT O'BRIEN

ARMCHAIR FICTION
PO Box 4369, Medford, Oregon 97501-0168

CHAPTER ONE

IT WAS scarcely a week before the God-forsaken little planet of Igakuro was due for its notoriously unbearable "scorch season," when the decrepit, incalculably ancient space cargo tramp ship moved dispiritedly into mooring at that planet's single, rust-eaten space wharf.

The name of the tramp space cargo carrier—scarcely discernible any longer through its paint scabbed, filthy hull—was *Venus Maiden;* the name of its Skipper, "Cap" Hutch.

While the glamorless space tub's obsolete electra-winches began laboriously to unload its twice-yearly supplies on Igakuro's wharfside, the skipper was first ashore with the consignment receipt papers.

Cap Hutch was as lumpy, as paint scarred, and as dirty as the spaceship he commanded. He was also almost as old. Rumor through interplanetary space trading posts had it that Cap had never bathed since *Venus Maiden* had received her last scrub down, and few people could remember that far back.

The afternoon of his stopover on Igakuro, coupled with the impending "scorch season," meant that the planet was already beginning to get a taste of the terrific heat that would soon descend upon it.

Perspiration cascaded down Cap Hutch's forehead as he moved quickly across the space wharf toward the shaded shelter of a small, *duralloy* dock shack standing some hundred yards off from the space mooring platform.

In his damp, pudgy right fist, Cap clutched his papers, and in his left a handkerchief with which he tried futilely to mop the waterfall from his bald forehead. Being exceedingly plump and more than a little seeped in Venusian whisky, the skipper of the *Venus Maiden* waddled precariously from side to side as he made for the dock shack.

By now the skipper was able to see the faint, almost scorched-out lettering inscribed on an equally bleached sign-board of *tawnalloy* above the door of the shack.

CARDIGAN & BENNETT
VARDIUM MINES FED. INC.

The space tramp skipper grunted as he saw the sign, put his head down once more, and hurried on.

"Hope Cardigan's off in his damn mines. Hope it's Bennett I have to break the news to," the skipper muttered wheezingly to himself.

By the time the skipper was three fourths of the distance from wharf to shack, he was wheezing badly, and by the time he finally clambered noisily up the steps of the shack, he could hardly stand erect. He leaned against the wall, knocked twice on the door and stood back to let those inside expend the energy of opening it for him.

STEPS sounded inside the shack, moving to answer Cap's knocking. The door opened, and a short, black haired, space-bronzed young man with incredibly wide shoulders stood there grinning at the wheezing Cap.

Although too spent to utter anything but a choked grunt, Cap Hutch thought: *Dammit—Cardigan. Why couldn't it have been Bennett?*

"Well, I'll be damned, Cap," the short, wide-shouldered young man exclaimed in sardonic amusement. "I haven't ever seen you hustle like this, even for a free quart of Venusian booze. What's up with that space sow of yours? Is she getting ready to explode?"

Still unable to talk, the tramp skipper shook his head and staggered into the small shack where he sank breathlessly grateful to a chair.

The big-shouldered young man closed the door behind them and walked across to a chair and a table where two glasses and a bottle stood waiting. Casually, he began to fill the glasses from the bottle, speaking as he did so.

"Native hooch," he commented. "Distilled in our lousiest planet swamp by one of my Igakuroan foremen. Ninety-nine and nine-tenths cosmic alki. If you had a hair left on that vacuum you call a head, it'd take it off with the first snort."

With a filled glass in either hand, the young man crossed to where the tramp skipper still sat wheezing and handed him one. Then he lifted his own aloft.

"Here's to twice-a-year, Cap. It's good I don't have to see more of you."

The young man raised his glass, drained it in a gulp, glanced at the empty bottom and smacked his lips.

"Lousy," he said, "but I've learned to love it."

Cap Hutch had finally caught his breath enough to speak. At least he opened his mouth to do so. Then he glanced at the glass in his hand, changed his mind, and lifted it to his lips. He took a long draught, downing almost half of the crimson liquid.

The young man watched him in amusement.

The skipper shuddered, made a face, looked reproachfully from the glass to the young man, then said, "You shoulda' warned me, Cardigan. I almost burned my tongue out."

"You looked like you needed it, Cap," young Cardigan said. "You almost broke your neck—in all this heat—getting over to the shack here. Mind if I ask you again what's up?"

Cardigan's question seemed to bring the skipper back jarringly to the point. He jerked back in his chair.

"Almost fergot!" he exclaimed, aghast.

Big-shouldered, short-statured Cardigan stepped over to the bottle on the table, refilled his own glass, and carried the bottle back in his other hand as he moved over to Cap Hutch again.

"Do you ever get to the point, Cap?" Cardigan demanded. "For the last time, what's up?" He frowned. "Something go wrong with any of the cargo consignments you had for me?" His voice took on a flat hardness, making the tramp spaceship skipper shake his head quickly.

"No, not on nothing like that, Cardigan. So help me. I never messed a consignment fer you yet, so help me. I—"

Cardigan cut him off impatiently.

"Get on with it, then."

"I got other kinda bad news fer you, Cardigan. I wanted to get here to the shack afore them, so's you'd be warned in advance." The skipper downed the rest of his drink with a practiced back snap of his head. Again he shuddered.

"Them?" Cardigan asked, the humor leaving his gray eyes. "What do you mean, *them?*"

CAP HUTCH squirmed his bulky body uneasily in his chair. He opened his mouth to say something, changed his mind, and gulped.

"Well?" Cardigan demanded impatiently. "Speak up. What's it all about? Who are *they?*"

The space tramp skipper took a deep breath.

"My passengers," he said.

Cardigan looked amused, then puzzled.

"Passengers? Don't tell me you're starting to buck the luxury liners' business by carrying passengers?"

Hutch grinned feebly at this amiable barb at the *Venus Maiden.*

"Hardly so, Cardigan," the skipper said.

"Where are your passengers headed for, Hutch?" Cardigan asked casually.

"That's what I was about to tell you," the older man wheezed. "They're getting off here."

Cardigan had been filling the tramp skipper's glass. Now, at the last words he paused, glaring stonily at Hutch.

"Repeat what you just said," he ordered flatly. "Repeat it slowly."

"They're getting off here," old Hutch mumbled apologetically. "Leastwise, they plan to."

Cardigan filled the rest of the tramp skipper's glass and handed it to him. The older man took it with a slightly trembling hand.

"They'll have to alter their plans, then," Cardigan said calmly. "We don't advertise for colonists and poachers on Igakuro. You could have told them that when they booked passage. It would have saved them a lot of trouble."

"You can't stop 'em from coming here, Cardigan," the space skipper protested weakly.

"Who in the hell says I can't?" Cardigan demanded. "All workable claims on this planet are ours, by law. Any interplanetary poachers will find themselves permanently dead if they try to—"

"They ain't poachers," the skipper broke in. "They got a written and signed habitation permit from the Interplanetary Zone Governor hisself to stay here as long as they like."

Young Cardigan stepped backward, thumped the bottle resoundingly on the old *duralloy* table.

"The hell you say!" he snapped.

"If you'll lemme tell you, Cardigan," the space skipper pleaded, "I'll explain why. You see, they ain't poachers, or traders, or anything like that. They're missionaries."

"Missionaries?" The word burst from young Cardigan's lips like a bombshell. He gaped incredulously at the skipper.

"S'truth, gawdamighty!" Cap exclaimed.

"Here? For Igakuro?" The amazement was still in the space-bronzed young trader's voice.

"For here. For Igakuro," the skipper said flatly.

"How many?" Cardigan demanded, after a second's pause.

Cap Hutch wet his lips, looked imploringly at the bottle on the table, then raised his hand, showing two fingers.

"Good lord," Cardigan said very disgustedly. "Two missionaries?"

"One ain't quite," said the space tramp's skipper. His eyes went back to the bottle, stayed there. "One is a—"

THE sound of footsteps ascending the steps to the shack porch sounded suddenly, then, cutting off the space skipper's sentence. Both men's glances went to the door. It was Cardigan who spoke first.

"That sounds like your passengers," he said grimly.

The footsteps had stopped now before the door. Then a swift, imperious tattoo sounded loudly upon it.

The skipper looked up at Cardigan. "I tried to tell you so's you'd be in the right frame of mind when you met 'em," he said.

"I'm in the right frame of mind," Cardigan said. He stepped to the door, his hand on the knob, turning to the skipper. "They got their passage back paid for?" he demanded.

The skipper opened his mouth to answer.

"They'd better have," Cardigan said grimly. He jerked the door open, stepping back as he did so.

Two people stood there in the doorway, a tall, lean, angular middle-aged man dressed in a severe black tunic, and a small, slim, blonde young woman whose features were half-hidden, inasmuch as her companion had taken a position slightly in front of her.

"How do you do?" the tall, black-tunicked stranger said. His face was expressionless, as expressionless as the deep voice that spoke the greeting. His somber dark eyes seemed to sweep the room and its occupants disapprovingly.

"Cardigan," stammered the space tramp skipper, scrambling to his feet foolishly. "This here is Parson Zender, the missionary, and his daughter, Miss Zender. Parson, this is Cleve Cardigan."

"Reverend Zender," the tall, unsmiling missionary corrected the skipper reprovingly; "not Parson."

Cardigan's expression was now erased of emotion, though he wore a polite smile.

"The skipper was just telling me about you, Reverend Zender," he said evenly. "Won't you and—ah—" he glanced at the slim blonde girl who was still half concealed behind the missionary, "—Miss Zender step inside?"

The pair stepped into the shack, and for the first time Cardigan clearly saw the girl. His eyes widened and he drew in his breath.

She was slim and blonde, as he'd observed at first; but her face, which had been half hidden, was a remarkably pleasant surprise. Oval, untinted by the artifice of cosmetics, it was nevertheless quite lovely. A small, pert, slightly tilted nose, hazel eyes, long-lashed, a soft, pretty mouth, all combined to show Cardigan that if this girl had the same name as the man beside her the resemblance between the two stopped there.

Cardigan tried to catch her eye, but he saw that her attention had been taken by the bottle on the table. He felt, rather than saw, her shocked appraisal of the object.

Reverend Zender had seen the bottle, but evidently deciding wisely to ignore it, turned his back on the table, not taking any of the four or five chairs in the room, and addressed Cardigan.

"Skipper Hutch has explained to you why we have come here?" the missionary demanded.

"Yes," said Cardigan. "Yes, he has."

"The Governor of this Interplanetary Zone informed me that you will be only too happy to establish some sort of quarters for Miss Zender and myself," the Reverend Zender said.

"Did he?" Cardigan asked noncommittally.

"He did," Reverend Zender said firmly. "I expect they will be suitable for—"

"—An overnight stay until the *Venus Maiden* pulls out again tomorrow morning," Cardigan broke in.

REVEREND ZENDER'S head snapped back. He stiffened.

"What was that, sir?

"Do you plan to stay on the planet here rather than aboard for tonight?" Cardigan asked amiably.

"I think you misunderstand me," the Reverend declared a bit testily, turning to glare at the skipper, "or that the skipper neglected to inform you fully of our plans here."

Cardigan seemed puzzled. He looked reprovingly at the haplessly squirming skipper.

"What's that, Cap? Are you staying over on Igakuro longer than a night? Staying two nights?" Cardigan asked.

"We are staying here permanently, sir," the Reverend Zender said. "Undoubtedly Skipper Hutch didn't inform you of that fact." He tried a smile, his first in Cardigan's presence. Cardigan suddenly realized why the Reverend Zender remained grave-faced. He didn't look any more pleasant when smiling.

Cardigan returned the smile.

"Why, Reverend, that's quite impossible. Didn't anyone tell you?" He paused. "We don't have room for you here, and this is no place, certainly, for women or missionaries. I'm really very sorry. Someone must have misguided you concerning this place."

The Reverend Zender was frowning. "This is Igakuro planet, is it not?" he demanded. "There are poor, Godless, native Igakuroan tribes on this planet and its chain of asteroids, are there not?"

"This is Igakuro," Cardigan answered evenly. "And as for Igakuroan natives living on this planet and some of its adjoining asteroids, of course they do. However, I don't believe you could pity them to the extent of calling them poor. And as for gods, they seem pretty well equipped. One swamp tribe I know of has at least a dozen gods right at the moment."

Wrath suddenly crackled in the cold dark eyes of the Reverend Zender.

"You have been making sport of me, sir!" he snapped.

Cardigan shook his head, leaned back against the table and picked up his glass and the bottle. He poured a glass of the crimson liquid casually as he spoke.

"No," he said quietly. "I haven't been making sport of you. I have just been telling you in as polite a fashion as possible that I'm top dog on this planet. I'm Cleve Cardigan. I've staked Igakuro for twenty-five years on a thoroughly legal Federation Claim. That gives me the right to drill as much *vardium* out of this planet in that time as I can, providing it's peddled to the Federation. That makes me pretty damned well boss around here, understand?"

"I still do not understand you, Cardigan," the Reverend Zender said. "Are you intimating we are unwelcome here?"

Cardigan filled his glass to the brim, put the bottle back on the table, looked up at the missionary.

"That's right," he said amiably. "You aren't wanted."

To Cardigan's astonishment as well, apparently, as that of the Reverend Zender, the girl broke in.

"Why?" she demanded suddenly. "Why aren't we welcome here, Mr. Cardigan?"

CARDIGAN still held the filled glass in his hand. He looked across the top of it almost abstractedly.

"I've stated two reasons," Cardigan said. "Two very excellent reasons. This is no place for a woman, and there is no room here for a missionary. I think those should be sufficient to make my point clear, don't you?" He looked sardonically at the girl.

She shook her head. "No, I don't," she said quietly. "In the first place, I have been with my father in many far flung space outposts. I stood the rigors of all of them. This shouldn't be different. Secondly, there is room for a missionary wherever decency and the word of God has not been spread. Igakuro is such a place."

Her head was tilted as she spoke, and her cheeks flushed slightly in anger, making Cardigan again conscious of her loveliness.

"Igakuro isn't any half-civilized Martian sub-planet, Miss," Cardigan said. "It's tougher than anything you or your father have ever encountered. The scorch season is just a week away, for one thing. Have you ever heard of Igakuro's scorch season?"

The Reverend Zender cut in.

"I never venture to establish a new mission on a planet about which I know nothing. I have studied the scant histories of Igakuro, its native inhabitants, the physical circumstances of the rigors of existence on it, a little of the native tongue—in short, all I could find. I am well acquainted with the nature of this planet."

"But this," said Cardigan dryly, "is the first time you've ever been here."

"Nevertheless, sir," said the Reverend Zender, "you cannot send us away. I have permits perfectly in order. You can refuse us assistance, if such be your kind, but we will stay."

Cardigan abruptly turned his back on the missionary and his daughter. He spoke to Cap Hutch.

"Pete Bennett will be here in a few minutes, Cap. You can look over the consignment papers with him. He'll sign them for you."

Cardigan stepped to the door. He turned to the man and girl.

"You're right about your legal permission to stay here on Igakuro, Reverend," he said coldly. "But you're also right about my refusal to help you. You'll have to get along as best you can, with no help from me, if you're foolish enough not to leave in the morning."

"We are not leaving," the Reverend Zender replied.

Cardigan shrugged.

"As you like. But at the moment you are standing on property that belongs to my company. I wish you'd get off as quickly as convenient."

The door slamming behind Cardigan shook the *duralloy* shack as if it had been tin...

CHAPTER TWO

THE smooth-hulled, black-sheened space cruisers that put in at Asteroid Eighty—a deserted and *vardium* drained spacial island in the Igakuro group—arrived there on the evening of the day the *Venus Maiden* had put in at Igakuro itself.

But these space cruisers (there were two in all) expected and found no welcoming delegations—native or Earthmen. The men aboard the cruisers had chosen Asteroid Eighty for the very reason that they knew it to be abandoned—and knew, also, that it was both within quick striking distance of Igakuro, and outside of even casual range of attention from that planet.

Several hours after disembarking, the men of the black-sheened cruisers had established themselves in the rusted and rotting mine shacks that still stood beyond the abandoned mooring wharf of the asteroid.

In the first of these shacks the leader of the group assembled six of his underlings for discussions that would forge the last of their plans into a striking weapon.

The leader of the group was tall, an Earthman well over six feet five inches. He was, in spite of his height, extraordinarily fat. His huge, corpulent body possessed long, thickly powerful arms, which gave him an ape-like appearance further carried out by his slight stoop, massive chest, and heavy, matted shock of black hair.

In the asteroid chains off Venus this brutish giant of a man had been called "The Strangler" by the harassed members of the Interspacial Border Patrol who had sought him so long and unsuccessfully for his many depredations.

Among his varied and often hideous crimes were his gang attacks on peaceful outpost trading colonies, native villages, and small, isolated Interspacial Border Patrol posts. These attacks, always in outnumbering force and with snake-like swiftness, had torn tribute of a hundred varieties from their victims. The trading colonies paid in their small wealth, the native villages in materials which trading Earthmen sought honestly, and the patrol posts in guns and ammunition for the restocking of the brigand band's arsenals. In common, they all paid in blood.

In contrast to the name bestowed on him by those who hunted him, the leader of this band was called, by his followers, "Satan." The name derived from his legal identification, "Saidun," to which he had been born, and had been bestowed on him by a space freebooter, long dead, who had been one of Satan's primary instructors when the brutish young man was but a novitiate in the field of space piracy.

Satan was no longer young, however, and though his black thatch of uncombed hair showed no gray, the villainous giant had passed forty.

His crew, consisting of twenty-three cutthroats of some seven planetary origins, were of varying ages, complexions, sizes, and temperaments. Each had been selected by Satan carefully, and each served his brigand master well.

THE six who met with the leader in the first of the abandoned mining shacks near the rotted mooring wharf of the asteroid were a fair sample of the rest.

Polo, the pockmarked Venusian renegade, was a squat, powerful, young man. Utterly hairless, he was distinguished by his completely toothless smile and jutting, rock-hard jaw.

Malveau, the most intelligent of the group, save Satan himself, was a tall, thin, mustached man with cold gray eyes, black hair, and the slim, pale hands of a woman. He was an Earthman.

Uska, the Junovian, was blind in one eye, and the ugly scar flesh that covered the eyeless gap did nothing to enhance his paste-complexioned, short-statured, doughy lumpiness. On occasions demanding his sideline specialty, Uska served as chief torturer.

Wenskus, another Earthman, was of medium stature, slim-shouldered, bespectacled, round-faced, unshaven. He had been discharged from the Interspacial Lines ten years previously when, as master of one of their largest luxury liners, he had deserted his post to let eight hundred passengers perish in an uncontrollable blaze. For Satan he served as an excellent space navigator and pilot.

Saturn was represented among the brigand lieutenants by Jekka, a saffron-skinned brute with the expressionless eyes and sadistic mouth of a killer. Next to Satan, Jekka was the burliest member of the band.

The last of Satan's lieutenants was a slim young Venusian who had deserted from his service with the Space Patrol. His name was Brona, and his knowledge of atomic cannon and ray gun repair was invaluable to the arsenal of the band.

Satan nodded to each of these lieutenants as they entered the shack and took places around the short, square table in the center of the room.

He waited until all were seated, and waited fully another minute after that, gazing at the blunt ends of his big fingers, before he spoke.

"There are only two of you here who realize the full purpose of our stop on this asteroid," he said. "Wenskus, who plotted our course of escape from the Venusian chain, and Malveau, who planned our next operations with me."

There was a momentary silence, broken by Uska, the partly blind Junovian.

"Iss not thiss sstop for hideout until border patrolss are sshaken?" he demanded.

Satan's big, heavy jowled features twisted in the semblance of a smile.

"That is what most of you were told," he said.

Polo ran his tongue over toothless gums in surprise. His pockmarked, Venusian features were expressionless, however, as he said, "Then what are the plans to be?"

Satan waited a moment before answering. Then he said cryptically, "Our biggest haul in some time."

THERE were no murmurs of surprise from his audience. His lieutenants merely continued to fix him with their unwinking stares, waiting for him to continue.

"We are safely beyond the reach of the annoying border patrols in the Venusian belt," Satan continued. "It is possible to assume that their intensified search for our cruisers will go on for another three or four months before they realize we are no longer operating in that territory. And when they realize we have taken to our heels, the reports of our work in this sector will begin to drift into their outposts here. By that time we shall move on again. And by that time, thanks to the job ahead of us, we shall have added more men and several more cruisers to our complement."

Satan paused to look around the circle at the faces of his lieutenants once more. They were still impassively attentive.

"Our haul this time," Satan went on, "will be *vardium*. *Vardium* in such quantity that certain sources in the Martian government will be delighted to pay us handsomely for it."

Now, at last, surprise flickered briefly on the faces of his lieutenants. Several turned, to exchange glances.

"Much of the *vardium* I speak of has already been mined and processed into *var-dust* for us," Satan went on. "The rest of it will be mined and processed before the scorch season in this belt is over. We can carry enough *var-dust* in one cruiser to bring a small fortune from the Martian sources I mentioned before. The Martians will pay heavily for the valuable munition-making soluble of which they have been deprived by the Interplanetary Federation." *

Uska, the Junovian, spoke up again.

"But who iss mad enough to mine thiss *vardium* for uss and processs it alsso ?"

Satan smiled. "Two young mining engineers on the central planet in this asteroid belt, Igakuro," he said. "Their names are Cardigan and Bennett. They've mined Igakuro for the past year without sending out any new shipments of *var-dust* to earth. The processed dust is stored in subterranean vaults, waiting a shipment two months after the scorch period comes on this belt. In the meantime they're working the natives extra shifts to mine and process more of the stuff before shipment time."

Brona, the slim young Venusian, spoke up now.

"What are the risks involved?" he asked. "Is Igakuro heavily armed? Are the patrols in this area heavy?"

Satan smiled again.

"There is a small detachment of Igakuroan natives that has been trained by Cardigan. They are poorly armed. Electra-rifles are their only weapons. I understand that several obsolete atomic cannon are concealed in small shacks on either side of the space-mooring wharf. Otherwise, they are empty-handed."

Polo spoke now.

----

* The "Interplanetary War I" was initiated by Mars against Earth, Venus, Juno, and Saturn; and was won by the latter. The victors then formed the Interplanetary Federation, from which Mars was omitted.—Ed.

"The guns from our cruisers could frighten the native guards back underground," he smirked.

"WE WILL not have to use the cruiser guns," Satan said. "They might destroy valuable equipment for the mining that must continue after we take over. No. It will be a simple matter to surprise and overpower the two Earthmen and whatever natives we encounter."

"Supposing the Earthmen resist?" asked the saffron-skinned Saturnian, Jekka. "Are they to be killed?"

"Not if it can possibly be prevented," said Satan. "They are to be kept alive to work the mines and oversee the processing of the *var-dust* until it is collected in sufficient quantity. Our operations might be considerably hampered if we had to tend to those details ourselves. The delay might be dangerous."

"And the natives?" asked the burly Jekka.

"Kill as many of them as you think necessary. They must be impressed with our superiority," Satan said. "Those devils must work those mines as if their lives depended on it. Their lives will, in fact, depend on it."

Polo put the next question. "When do we strike?"

"We start for Igakuro tomorrow afternoon," said the leader. We will reach there shortly after darkness has fallen the following day. The place should be in our hands in less than an hour after that."

"How long we sstay on Igakuro?" Uska demanded.

"A month should prove sufficient," Satan said. "The scorch season will be ending, then, and the danger of patrol visits will increase. We can be out of this zone and en route to Mars before suspicion is aroused."

A murmur of approval greeted this. Satan stood up. Under the black bushes of his brows, his pale eyes glinted coldly.

"You can spread the word of our plans to the rest," he said. He turned to the tall, thin, black-moustached Earthman, Malveau. "Wait a moment. I've something more to discuss with you, Malveau," he ordered.

The other five lieutenants rose on this obvious signal that the discussion was at an end. They filed out of the shack until at last there was only Satan and Malveau.

The massive, brutish leader turned to the slender, cold-eyed Earthman. He grinned.

"It didn't occur to any of them to question the transportation problem we'll encounter when we use one of the cruisers to carry the *var-dust*," he said.

Malveau grinned briefly in reply, then said, "It won't occur to the others, either. But if it does, I have a simple explanation ready to assure them. You've made the selections of those who will be left on Igakuro and those who will be taken with us?"

Satan nodded.

"The choices were fairly easy. Our band should be considerably improved by the elimination of some dead timber. And, of course, the splitting of the profit on this venture will be much more simple among an even dozen of us, rather than twenty-four."

"We shall not leave them on Igakuro alive?" Malveau asked.

"And run the risk that a patrol ship might stop on the planet and clap them in custody?" Satan was amused. "Certainly not. We can't risk anything of the sort. Those twelve unfortunate selections I've made must be snuffed out before we leave Igakuro. It is the only sensible way, and it prevents any possibility of talk."

MALVEAU pulled a thin, black Junovian cigar from his tunic pocket. He bit off the end with his white, sharp teeth, lighted it, and blew a cloud of smoke ceilingward.

"Are you quite certain that your reports on the condition at Igakuro are correct?" he asked.

"Naturally," Satan said. "My Martian source had it all checked very thoroughly by an agent posing as a member of the *Venus Maiden*—that's a space tramper that carries supplies to the planet twice yearly—on that tub's last visit to Igakuro six months ago."

"Then the space tramp you mention should be due there at some time within this week," said Malveau, "if it makes a twice-yearly trip to the planet."

"Certainly," the massive Satan asserted. "It is moored there at this very moment. It will leave tonight, perhaps, but more likely tomorrow."

Malveau's eyebrows lifted.

"What does it carry?"

"Nothing of importance," Satan shrugged. "It would not be worth while to seize it."

"But a small crew, one cruiser, could do the job—" Malveau began.

His leader cut him off. "You forget, Malveau," Satan declared, "that our operations are no longer on such petty scale. We no longer need bother with such small loot as the *Venus Maiden* would provide."

Malveau smiled faintly.

"We seem really to be branching into bigger fields, my friend," he observed.

Satan sat down, running his huge hand through the thick, tangled black shock of his hair. His eyes, for an instant, glittered more coldly than before. The expression on his face was momentarily far-off.

"If we deliver the *var-dust* as agreed to the Martians," he said, "we will not have to worry any longer about meager operations. There will be many more tasks they can find for us, for equally tremendous compensation."

Malveau's eyebrows went up again, but he said nothing.

Satan smiled to himself, then looked up at his moustached lieutenant, grinning.

"We make no mistake, eh?" he said…

CHAPTER THREE

FOR fully a minute after Cardigan's departure, there was an uncomfortable silence inside the shack. Finally the Reverend Zender turned to stare coldly at the bottle and glass on the table.

Cap Hutch spoke.

"I told you, Parson," he said. "This Cardigan is young, but he's tough, obstinate. He don't want nobody on Igakuro except himself, his partner, and the natives who work his *vardium* mines for him."

The girl spoke. "Obviously, he isn't a strongly religious person," she said. "He seems hardly God-fearing."

"Cardigan," the skipper observed wryly, "don't fear nobody. Anyone in the interplanetary space-trading bunch can tell you that. He fought his way to where he is, from the time he was sixteen, in ten short years. Shipped aboard his first space tramper when his folks was killed. Worked as roustabout all over space. They usta' kid him about his height. But he had shoulders that were wider than any six-footer's I ever seen. Used 'em, too, as well as his fists and an atomic pistol he could shoot the whiskers off a cat with."

The Reverend Zender took his eyes from the bottle and glass on the table. He spoke to the tramp space skipper.

"You mentioned before that he has a partner with him in this *vardium* mining venture on Igakuro. I think I heard Cardigan call him Bennett. Is he of the same stripe?"

"Oh, Pete Bennett," Cap Hutch said. "Yup. He's Cardigan's partner. Youngster, too, this Bennett. About the same age as Cardigan. Mebbe a little older, though, mebbe closer to thirty. He's a lot more easy-going than Cardigan.

Tall, slim feller. As blonde as Cardigan is brunette. Mebbe he'll give you and your daughter a hand."

"Would Cardigan permit him to?" the girl asked.

"Cardigan couldn't say no," Cap Hutch declared. "They're fifty-fifty partners here, though Bennett thinks Cardigan's tops and does about the way Cardigan wants in everything."

They hadn't heard the light tread mounting the steps of the shack, and now all three were surprised as the door of the shack opened suddenly, revealing a tall, tow-headed young man who grinned at them quizzically.

"Hello there," the new arrival said. He saw Cap Hutch then and added amiably, "Hiya, Skipper. Looking for me? Where's Cleve?"

Cap Hutch rose, smiling. "Well, Petey Bennett! I was just telling this lady and gentleman, here, you'd be willing to help 'em out, since yer partner jest walked out inna huff."

The Reverend Zender stepped into the conversation, quickly identified himself and his daughter, then said, "Your partner, Mr. Cardigan seems somehow unwilling to accommodate us on Igakuro at all, sir. The reception he gave us was not at all pleasant. He just left, after telling us to keep off your company's property if we intend to stay here."

PETE BENNETT looked from the missionary to his daughter. The big white grin he gave her was appreciative.

"Do you intend to stay on in spite of Cardigan's warnings?" Bennett asked. He spoke to the father; although his eyes were still on the girl.

"We do, sir," said the Reverend Zender grimly.

Pete Bennett took his eyes from the girl and shifted his amiable grin to her father.

"Cardigan is a fine chap, Reverend," Bennett said. "Don't draw any hasty conclusions about him from your first meeting. I'm sure he harbors nothing personal against either you or your daughter in not wanting you to stay on here."

"How decent of him," the girl declared with soft sarcasm.

"You see, sir," Bennett said, still speaking to the father but grinning briefly to the girl again, "Cardigan has had a slightly different life than most chaps his age. He's had to fight for everything he's gained. He doesn't hate religion, really, he just feels that any philosophy that teaches that one should turn the other cheek and live in meekness, and all that sort of thing, is haywire. Personally, I'm aware he's off base in that reasoning. However, he'll come around, if you're intent on staying on here."

The Reverend Zender extended his hand.

"Then you will assist us, sir?" he asked. "In spite of your partner's attitude?"

Bennett took the missionary's hand in a hearty clasp.

"Sure thing," he said. "If you've legal permission to be here, and are determined to stay, we can't very well act like barbarians to the only other earth people on Igakuro. Cardigan, as I said, will come around. In the meantime, I'll do whatever I can to fix you up with what you need. You can count on my half of the company property as being accessible to your needs." He grinned, then, turning to Cap Hutch. "Got those consignment papers ready, Skipper?"

The Reverend Zender took his daughter by the arm. At the door, he turned to young Bennett and bowed with stately formality.

"Thank you again, Mr. Bennett. My daughter and I will return to the spaceship to remove our luggage in the meantime. Perhaps you could think of some quarters for us by then?"

"Certainly," Bennett said. "You'll stay somewhere around the stockade in which Cardigan and I are living. I'll be down to the space wharf as soon as I have this business with the skipper settled."

The Reverend and his daughter left.

The door no sooner closed behind them than young Bennett stepped to the bottle on the table and poured himself a stiff hooker of the native whisky. He turned to Cap Hutch.

"Your glass is empty, Cap. Cardigan been holding back on you? Fill up and have a snort, then we'll get to those papers."

For a man of his age and girth, Cap Hutch moved from his chair to the bottle on the table with amazing alacrity...

OUTSIDE, on the porch of the *duralloy* dock consignment shack, the Reverend Zender and his attractive daughter blinked in the white-hot glare that beat mercilessly down on Igakuro.

"He seems like a decent sort, Father," the girl observed. "Very obliging, in contrast to that Cardigan person."

"Cardigan," the Reverend Zender said, his mouth tight, "seems more in need of salvation than any of the natives we shall work with."

"Mr. Bennett and the space skipper told us much that might explain him," the girl ventured.

The Reverend Zender shook his head forebodingly. "Scarcely. There is little excuse for such an attitude in a man blessed by birth with a civilized status in this universe."

They started down the steps of the shack, and, less than an instant later, almost collided headlong with a tall, sinewy massive, half-naked creature who had come around the side of the shack in a great hurry and started up the same steps they were descending.

Both the Reverend Zender and his daughter stepped back instinctively in surprise. The creature with whom they had almost collided also stepped back, looking up at them from a lower step a little stupidly. He had a low, wide skull, completely hairless. His nose was small, almost a round blob in the middle of his moon face. His lips were thick, his eyes round, red, and staring. His skin was a verdant green hue.

Zender was the first to speak. "Why," he declared, "an Igakuroan!"

The Igakuroan was staring at Zender and his daughter with almost equal surprise. His interest seemed especially centered on the girl; his round eyes moving from her to her father and back again.

"Who are you, my good man?" the Reverend Zender asked. "Do you have a name?"

The massive, half-stripped Igakuroan didn't answer. He continued to stare at the two, his red, round eyes flickering weirdly against the green of his face.

"Try his dialect, Father," the girl suggested.

The Reverend Zender hesitated a moment. He summoned up what he knew of his scanty fund of Igakuroan dialectics, then haltingly rephrased his question in the native's tongue.

Still the Igakuroan didn't answer. He continued to stare at the two.

The shack door opened behind the missionary and his daughter. They heard Pete Bennett's voice.

"Come on, Torgan. What's been keeping you?"

The massively muscled Igakuroan stepped around the missionary and his daughter and started up the steps, looking back over his shoulder at the two earth people as he did so.

"Coming, Bennett Boss," the Igakuroan who'd been called Torgan said gutturally. "Stop to look, see two new Earthmen. Who they?"

The Reverend Zender suddenly flushed crimson. His daughter smiled faintly, touched her father's arm.

"We'd better get our baggage from the spaceship, Father," she suggested.

They moved down the steps and started toward the wharf...

CHAPTER FOUR

WHEN Cleve Cardigan left the dock shack, he went directly to the combination compound-stockade some three miles from the mooring wharf, where the Cardigan-Bennett Company had its headquarters, and where he and his partner had established living premises for themselves.

During the three-mile journey to the compound-stockade, the terrain, which lay between there and the wharf-mooring location, became increasingly heavy with an *astera-tropical* jungle growth. Cardigan and Bennett had originally decided on the location of their headquarters because it was conveniently established in regard to the small shaft mines they'd first bored within a ten mile radius of it, and also centrally located near one of the largest Igakuroan tribal camps from which they drew their mining labor supply.

Now, even though the shaft borings were being carried out in increasingly more distant locations, Cardigan and his partner had decided to keep their compound-stockade headquarters and living establishment where it was, since it continued to be valuable in proximity to the space landing wharf of Igakuro.

Arriving a little later at the compound stockade, Cardigan, still angrily disturbed over the argument he'd had with the missionary and his daughter, had nevertheless managed to force himself into getting some sleep, before starting on his every-other-night inspection of their mines lying back in the *astera-tropical* jungles.

Cardigan and his partner alternated nightly on these inspection trips of the mines. And because of the approach of Igakuro's "scorch season," during which time they would be forced to operate their mines entirely at night, these trips were now increasingly important in the gradual establishment of night-operating mining crews.

When Cardigan had had sufficient sleep, consequently, he rose and attired himself in the *astera-tropical* garb needed for his inspection tour, and set out into the jungle slightly before dusk.

It was due to his absence, and the additional fact that the Reverend Zender and daughter were unable to get their luggage unloaded from the *Venus Maiden* until almost dusk, that Cardigan was unaware of his partner's establishing the missionary and the girl in the compound-stockade until almost noon of the next day, when he came back from his inspection.

When he came up the trail to the compound-stockade, in view of the first of the native huts that flanked it, Cardigan encountered the girl.

Cardigan was tired, mire-splashed, and unshaven. His nerves were none too settled from an unusually troublesome inspection round. Over his shoulder was slung an electra-rifle, and strapped to one side, an atomic pistol.

The girl had just come from one of the native huts. She wore a white tunic that, in spite of the severity of line, wasn't quite able to conceal the slim, appealing youthfulness of a decidedly attractive figure.

BUT Cardigan noticed none of this. He felt only a sudden swift surge of rage. He stood there in the trail as the girl, seeing him, started smilingly in his direction.

"Just back from the mines, Mr. Cardigan?" the girl called, still moving toward him. "Mr. Bennett set my father and me up in one of your extra compounds. I hope you'll forgive us, but we couldn't sleep on the docks, you know."

Cardigan still didn't speak, until the girl was several yards from him.

"I thought I made myself clear yesterday as to what I thought about you and your father's staying on?" Cardigan demanded then.

The smile left the girl's face. She stopped.

"I thought you'd at least be a good sport about it, now that you realize we're determined to stay."

"Is the *Venus Maiden* still in dock?" Cardigan asked.

The girl nodded.

"Then you and your father still have time to get yourselves back aboard her," Cardigan said.

"We have no intention of doing so," the girl answered.

Cardigan started to say something, then clamped his jaws shut, gave the girl a savagely angry glare, and stepped around her. He stamped off down the path to his compound in silence...

PETE BENNETT was playing a game of solitaire on a porch table when Cardigan stamped up the steps to their compound.

" 'Allo, Cleve," he said amiably. "How was the tour?"

Cardigan unslung his electra-rifle, unbuckled the belt which held his atomic pistol holster, and dropped the weapons into a corner. He turned to Bennett, both hands on his hips, eyes filled with disgust and anger.

"I thought you'd be out at prayer meeting, Pete!" he snapped.

Bennett grinned at this and continued to turn over cards in search of a red Jack for a black Queen.

"There haven't been any yet, Cleve," he answered casually. "But we ought to sit in on the Reverend Zender's first one, at that, don't you think?"

"The hell I think!" Cardigan exploded.

Bennett found a red Jack for the black Queen and quite triumphantly placed it in order.

"I was beginning to think that would never turn up," he said.

Cardigan's lips worked, but he cut off the words that started to them.

"To hell with your game!" he snorted. Then he turned away and stamped off the porch into the compound.

Pete Bennett smiled for a moment, then put down the cards, rose, and followed Cardigan inside. He found his partner stripping his soaked and dirty tunic shirt from his wide, muscular young torso.

Bennett stood at the door to Cardigan's room, watching him with the same amiable smile on his lips. Then he said, "Come on, Cleve. Snap out of it. You're acting like a five year old kid."

Cardigan didn't say anything. He sat down on the edge of his bunk and began to doff his insulated vardium boots. He grunted and cursed through the process, still paying no attention to Bennett.

"You're making yourself ridiculous, old man," Bennett said easily. "We've no right to throw the Zenders off. The only rights that are exclusively ours on this planet are the *vardium* rights. Since there's nothing that can be done to get them off, and since they'll be the only other earth people on Igakuro, we might as well make the best of it."

Cardigan removed his right boot with a vicious tug. He let it thud heavily to the *duralloy* floor, then glared up at his partner.

"You have it all figured out, haven't you?" he asked with thick sarcasm.

Bennett shrugged. "Hell, Cleve. You figure it out some other way."

Cardigan stood up. "All right," he said, suddenly calm. "I'll tell you another way I've figured it out. I'll tell you things you should be bright enough to figure out yourself."

"Sure, Cleve, go ahead," Bennett said.

"Number one—and of first importance," Cardigan began, holding up one finger. "This is no time of year for us to be involved with outside trouble, of any sort. The scorch is coming on, and it's a tough enough job mining our *vardium* and keeping the natives in hand during that period under any circumstances. That reason would hold against the desirability of strangers here no matter who they were. You understand that?"

"Sure," Bennett began, "but—"

CARDIGAN cut his partner off, holding up a second finger beside his first, and plunging on.

"Reason number two," he said, "is idiotically clear, and it is tied to the first reason. I said strangers—no matter who they were, mind you—are poison on this planet now. These strangers are double poison. They're missionaries."

"Wait a minute—" Bennett began again.

But Cardigan ignored the interruption. He continued.

"They are here with one purpose—to stick their noses into the affairs and lives of our natives."

"We don't own the natives," Bennett smiled.

"No!" Cardigan snapped. "But we pay their wages and keep them healthy with our medicines, and clean and somewhat sanitary in the compounds we've had constructed for them."

"And they," Bennett observed, "mine our *vardium* for us in return. It isn't as one-sided as you like to think it is, Cleve."

Cardigan snorted. "You oughta' run for mayor of this place, Pete. You're really the friend of the common peeeeeepull!"

Bennett sighed, then shrugged and grinned.

"All of this doesn't get anywhere, Cleve," he said amiably. "The missionaries are here and there's nothing we can do about that part of it. And as far as I can see, there's nothing we can do about them during their stay here. In view of that, why not act sensible and treat them humanly?"

Cardigan scowled, frowned.

"They're here, all right. And there isn't anything we can do to throw them off. But there might be something we could do to make them want to leave."

"Such as?" Bennett asked.

Cardigan scowled again. "I'm not sure, yet. But I'll think of something. I can promise you that."

Bennett shrugged.

"Don't depend on my helping you scheme against them," he said. He started to turn away. Cardigan's words made him pause.

"Is it because of the girl?" Cardigan sneered. "The sight of a pretty face and a trim figure too much for you?"

Bennett looked at his partner speculatively a moment. He didn't smile as he answered.

"Don't be an ass!" he said.

Cardigan's eyebrows lifted in sardonic triumph.

"So it is the dame, eh?"

Bennett turned and left the doorway without saying anything more. Cardigan heard him clumping out onto the veranda. He grinned humorously and snorted.

CHAPTER FIVE

THE blue murkiness of Igakuroian twilight had enveloped the veranda of the compound when Cardigan arrived there for the evening meal several hours later.

Cap Hutch, Bennett, the missionary Zender, and his daughter were already seated at the table which had been improvised to seat the unexpected guests.

Bennett sat at one end of the table, and had left the chair at the opposite end unoccupied for his partner. The missionary's daughter sat on Bennett's right, the father on his left. Cap Hutch, looking considerably uncomfortable, sat to the left of the Reverend.

Cardigan took his seat silently, not acknowledging the presence of the girl and her father with so much as a nod.

Torgan, the massive, green-skinned, red-eyed Igakuroan was supervising the service for the table. A small, thin native did the actual waiting and menial chores.

The silence, which had been created by Cardigan's entrance, was broken suddenly by Bennett, who turned to the girl and said, "You were telling us about one of the missions your father and you established in the Junovian chain," he said.

Cardigan looked up sharply, glowered, and snorted. His blond partner ignored him and continued, as Cardigan turned his attention to the food on his plate.

The girl seemed to hesitate an instant as Bennett said, "I was interested. I wish you'd continue."

"That's about all there was to tell," the girl said softly. "It proved to be a great success, and won the natives over

137

admirably. Father and I didn't have the slightest trouble with them thereafter."

"Miss Zender was telling us about the time she and her father ran into a little trouble with some natives on the Junovian asteroid chain, Cleve," Bennett said amiably. "It seems that a chief of one of the Junovian interior tribes was—"

Cardigan's cold sentence cut his partner off.

"I'm not interested in missionary twaddle," he said. "The next thing you know we'll be shown illustrated slides and a plate will be passed in collection."

The silence was electric. The Reverend Zender broke it. The sound of his knife clattering to the table was like an electra-cable clattering to the deck of a space tube.

The missionary rose, glaring at Cardigan.

Cardigan looked up at him, meeting the stare unwinkingly.

"We will not trouble you any longer, sir," said the Reverend Zender. He was controlling himself with the greatest of difficulty, his voice shaking with rage and humiliation. He turned to his daughter. "Come, Carol. We'll find someplace on this planet where we will be less of an annoyance to Mr. Cardigan."

The girl was white-faced, sharing her father's anger and hurt. The look she gave Cardigan was cold, venomous. She rose from the table and followed her father to the door of the veranda.

Cardigan looked sardonically amused. He finally replied to the missionary's declaration.

"That will suit me just fine," he said.

BENNETT was on his feet by the time the girl and her father were at the door. His amiable tolerance had gone. The look he gave his partner was one of disgusted anger.

"Please, Reverend Zender, Miss Zender—" he began.

"I'm sorry, Mr. Bennett," said the missionary. "You have been very kind. But Mr. Cardigan's hostility leaves us no other choice."

The missionary and his daughter stepped out into the darkness. Bennett turned on Cardigan, his lips tight in anger. Wordlessly, he glared at his partner.

Cardigan met Bennett's stare unflinchingly, challengingly.

"You ignorant lout!" Bennett snapped at last.

Cardigan laughed, and turned his attention back to his food.

The door slammed behind Bennett as he left the veranda in pursuit of the missionary and his daughter.

Cardigan looked up at Hutch, the sale survivor of the scene. He grinned.

"You like to finish the meal with me, Cap?" he asked.

The skipper of the tramp spaceship was flushed, uncomfortable, perspiring. He mopped his brow with a dirty handkerchief. He sighed and managed a feeble grin.

"You sure are some host, Cardigan. Got any of that atomic hooch on hand? I need a stiff jolt."

Cardigan looked up at Torgan. The big Igakuroan had watched the scene impassively.

"Break out a bottle of the best, Torgan," he said. "The wet blanket has been lifted from the party."

Torgan grinned lopsidedly and went away to get the liquor. Cardigan turned back to Hutch.

"I think maybe you could wait around another day, Hutch. You stand a good chance of having a couple of passengers to take back to where they came from."

The tramp spaceship skipper tried to look neutral.

"I got some rocket trouble I could layover to repair," he said. "It might be a good idea if I took this chance to attend to it, I think."

Cardigan laughed. "I think so, too," he said.

There was a momentary silence. Torgan appeared with a bottle and glasses. He set them before Cardigan. Cardigan broke the seal on the bottle, poured the scorching liquid into two tumblers, and handed one to Hutch.

"Here's to bigger and better missionaries—on other planets," he toasted.

Hutch imitated the gesture of his host, raising his glass and tossing off half the liquid with a snap of his head. He put the glass back on the table, making a face and shuddering.

"It don't seem good to see any ruckus between you and Pete Bennett," the tramp skipper observed. "It ain't at all like either of you. You two was always the best of buddies."

Cardigan scowled, tossed off the rest of his drink. He stared at Hutch, lips pursed thoughtfully.

"Didn't I tell you missionaries make nothing but trouble?" he demanded.

Hutch opened his mouth, as if to refute the reasoning behind Cardigan's statement. Then he decided that it would not be the better part of discretion to remind the wide-shouldered, stocky young man that all the trouble caused to date had been his own doing.

"Didn't I tell you that?" Cardigan repeated belligerently, refilling his glass.

"Yeah," Hutch said noncommittally. "Yeah, you certainly did, Cardigan. You certainly did."

"Of course I did," Cardigan snapped. "Drink up. You're falling behind me in this bout."

"This gonna be a bout?" asked Hutch with quickened interest.

"You're damned right it is," Cardigan promised. "Come on. Drink up."

Cap Hutch swallowed the liquor left in his glass and extended it to Cardigan. The young man filled it to the brim again, and grinned.

"To hell with Bennett," Cardigan said.

Cap Hutch was busy working on his second drink…

WHEN Pete Bennett came back to their compound considerably later in the evening, he saw Torgan clearing a litter of glasses and bottles from the table on the veranda.

"Where's Boss Cardigan?" Bennett demanded.

"Cardigan Boss on *Venus Maiden*.

Cardigan Boss and Hutch Boss damn drunk. Take plenty bottles. Go drink on spaceship, they say."

Bennett kept his anger from the Igakuroan foreman. But his lips were tight in rage as he stalked through the compound into his bedroom.

When Bennett had dressed for bed, he sat on the edge of his bunk for over an hour, smoking and frowning alternately. He rose, then, checked his *astera-tropical* gear for his trip to the mines in the interior the following day.

Some fifteen minutes later Bennett stretched out on his bunk, finished another smoke, and mentally cursed the stubborn streak in his partner until he fell asleep.

Cardigan staggered into the compound some six hours later. Early Igakuroan dawn was breaking, and the dark-haired, wide-shouldered young man was exceptionally drunk. Too drunk to remove his clothes before falling into a dead slumber across his bunk.

When Bennett rose and donned his *astera-tropical* attire, an hour after that, he stopped in Cardigan's room long enough to pick up his partner's electra-rifle, two or three other small items of equipment, and to scratch a brief note on a pad atop the table beside the bunk.

Bennett left, then, and went out onto the veranda where the tireless Torgan had breakfast waiting. The blond young mining engineer ate his morning snack in silence, the Igakuroan foreman watching him curiously.

"Any talk for Cardigan Boss?" Torgan asked, as Bennett finished the breakfast and started toward the veranda door.

Bennett hesitated a moment, then shook his head.

"None, Torgan. I'll be back from this inspection stretch early tomorrow morning, if he should ask. The Number Twenty *vardium* shafts need some extra supervision."

The big Igakuroan nodded solemnly.

"I tell Cardigan Boss same," he said. Bennett left the compound. Moments later he was striding down the trail into the thick vegetation that fringed the swamplands of Igakuro...

HALF a day away from Asteroid Eighty, the crews of the twin, black-sheened space cruisers were busy on the decks of the swiftly moving vessels. Satan and Malveau were breakfasting while delivering orders to lieutenants concerning the preparation and armament necessary for the raid.

The brief rehearsal for the raid would take place, verbally, in Satan's compartment, within a few hours. And a few hours after that, Igakuro would come into view.

Malveau held a thin Junovian cigar between his white teeth, a small cup of Venusian coffee almost daintily in his slender, woman-like hand. He was smiling at an observation just made by his leader.

Satan, busily gorging his great, obese body, talked as he munched food.

"Those we have decided to eliminate later will comprise the first of our raiding party to land," he said. "Should some of them be stupid enough to be killed, we shall be saved considerable trouble later." He paused. "In fact, I think it might be wise if we planned the raid so as to make it almost inevitable that some of that first group in the landing party are eliminated."

Malveau took the thin cigar from his teeth, sipped his coffee, and chuckled.

"An excellent idea," he agreed.

"Uska," Satan went on, around a mouthful of food, "shall be designated to lead that first group."

"Uska?" Malveau was surprised. Satan nodded. "I have noticed a certain tendency on the part of the Junovian to think too much for himself. I am not at all sure that his loyalty could be trusted should he have a chance to bring the men in behind him."

"Surely you don't think that thick-witted Junovian would contemplate challenging your leadership?" Malveau demanded.

Satan stopped munching food long enough to smile.

"I make it a point to keep in touch with the trends of—ah—thought among my men," he said. "I have heard it said that Uska has made several questioning statements on several occasions."

"Questioning statements?"

Satan nodded.

"It seems he questioned our leaving the scene of Venusian operations so soon," the leader declared. "It seems his greed was not at all balanced with good judgment or faith in my decisions."

Malveau was wordless. He put down his Venusian coffee, put the thin Junovian cigar back between his white teeth. He looked at Satan. The leader glanced up sharply, smiling ambiguously.

"Anyone," said Satan, "who thinks himself clever enough to take control from my hands has only to try."

Malveau didn't say anything. The smile he essayed was only a reasonably passable one. His cold gray eyes were, momentarily, clouded and shifty.

Satan chuckled and went on eating...

CHAPTER SIX

CLEVE CARDIGAN'S head was heavy and aching, and his tongue was coated as if by cellucotton. He blinked uncomfortably through red-rimmed, burning eyes and looked around.

He was in his room, on his bunk. He was fully dressed and his tunic was wrinkled and dirty. He groaned and sat up.

The noise of his feet striking the floor must have told Torgan that Cardigan had awakened, for the massive Igakuroan appeared at the door of the squat, wide-shouldered young man's room an instant later, a glass in his hand.

"Cardigan Boss pick up," said Torgan. He handed Cardigan the glass.

Cardigan shuddered as he drained the contents. He was never at all certain what mixture Torgan concocted to bring him out of his hangovers from native whisky, but it tasted utterly foul.

Cardigan handed the glass back to Torgan.

"Breakfast," he said. "Now."

Torgan nodded and left.

The heaviness was leaving Cardigan's head, and his eyes burned less. The perspective of the room regained normalcy. Torgan's pick-up was working according to schedule.

Cardigan rose, sticking out his tongue and touching it with his forefinger. He made an expression of distaste. Then he grinned, wondering how the skipper of the *Venus Maiden* was feeling.

As Cardigan was discarding his rumpled, slept-in tunic for fresh garments he noticed the note on the table beside his bed. It was from Bennett, stating merely that he was starting early for his inspection junket because of the necessity to make another supervision check on the Number Twenty shafts. It was signed merely with Bennett's initials.

Cardigan crumpled the note into a ball, tossed it carelessly into a corner and continued with his dressing.

When Cardigan stepped onto the veranda the sunlight was glazing, exceptionally hot, indicating another day closer to the scorch season. He sat down to the breakfast Torgan had had prepared for him, and asked the massive Igakuroan what time it was.

"Noon?" Cardigan blinked in answer to Torgan's statement. "Good Lord—half the day shot. The *Venus Maiden* still in mooring?"

Torgan nodded.

As Cardigan ate his breakfast he determined to seek out the missionary and his daughter immediately afterward. He would indicate to them in no uncertain terms that they would have their last chance to leave Igakuro on the *Venus Maiden.* He wondered where they had put up for the night. Probably in the compound Bennett had been stupid enough to give them. It was unlikely that the Reverend's indignation had gone as far as refusal to use any of the company property.

THE breakfast served to stabilize Cardigan against the effects of his drinking bout even further, and he rose from the table feeling much better.

"Earthman, Earthwoman," Cardigan said to Torgan. "They sleep inside stockade, in compound?"

The big Igakuroan looked puzzled. Cardigan repeated his question, adding that he wished to know in which compound Bennett Boss had put the earth people.

"Far side stockade," Torgan said. "They not there now."

Cardigan frowned.

"Where are they? Are they meddling around in the native huts outside the stockade?"

Torgan shook his head.

"They leave early morning. Dawn not break."

Cardigan was surprised, then suspicious.

"With Bennett Boss?" he asked.

Again Torgan shook his head.

"Before Bennett Boss go. They go inside." Torgan waved his hand to indicate the depths of the jungle and swamplands.

Cardigan's expression went hard.

"They went into the interior? Did you tell Bennett Boss? That why Bennett Boss leave early?"

Torgan shook his head. "I no tell Bennett Boss. Bennett Boss no ask Torgan."

Cardigan cursed.

"Those damned fools!"

Torgan shook his head.

"I watch them go. I think not wise. I not person to tell them. They alone."

Cardigan stood there a moment, his face angry, his manner indecisive. He began to swear, and continued to do so uninterruptedly for over a minute. Then his lips went tight. He shrugged.

"To hell with them," he said. "It's their worry, not mine. Maybe it's best. It's an easy way to get rid of them. And, at any rate, it's a damned sight better that Bennett didn't find out the damned fools were pulling up stakes."

He turned to Torgan. "Don't say anything about this to Skipper Boss on *Venus Maiden*, understand?"

Torgan nodded slowly, puzzledly. Cardigan Boss was sometimes very hard to understand. But the moods of the Earthman were no concern of Torgan's. What Cardigan Boss or Bennett Boss commanded, Torgan did gladly...

ABOARD the *Venus Maiden*, the fat little skipper of the tramp spaceship stared moodily at the breakfast brought into his quarters by the steward. Hutch had a blinding hangover, and his only emotion was remorse.

"I'm an old ass," he told himself ruefully, "to think I can keep up with a two-fisted young rioter like Cardigan."

He shuddered, and mopped his damp forehead.

The *Venus Maiden's* scrawny space-radio operator, attired in a worn, incredibly dirty uniform tunic, appeared at the tramp skipper's door, then, saluting sloppily.

"Well, Suran," Hutch demanded irritably, "what is it?"

Suran looked worried, but he took time deciding on his opening line. Finally he blurted out, "I was making *vizascreen* testings," said Space Radio Operator Suran, "and I picked up the disturbance shadows."

Cap Hutch glared impatiently at Suran.

"What in thunder you talking about? What disturbance shadows?"

"On the screen, sir," said Suran. "The disturbance shadows on the *vizascreen*. I was making tests, beaming the screen out to see what distance I could get from it, and these two shadow disturbances began to blot in and out on it."

Hutch's irritation formed in sarcasm.

"Two disturbance shadows, eh?" he said. "And what were they, Martian battleships?"

Suran flushed.

"The outlines seemed like they were cruiser-size ships, sir, commercial design. But they could be interspacial patrol craft on the prowl."

Cap Hutch's sarcasm and irritation vanished immediately. He pushed aside the tray from which he had been eating breakfast, rising from the edge of his bunk.

"Are you sure? I mean, are you sure that there could possibly be interspacial patrol craft prowling around?"

The space radio officer nodded worriedly.

"That's why I came right to you, sir," he said. "I know we don't want any patrol officers snooping around the cargo of the *Venus Maiden*. That smuggled shipment bound for Juno—the one we picked up in Venus—could get us all into a lot of trouble, sir."

The skipper of the *Venus Maiden* was pale.

"Mebbe I better have a look-see at that *vizascreen,*" he said shakily.

The skipper of the *Venus Maiden* stood beside his space radio officer several minutes later, staring at the glowing pink surface of the *vizascreen* in the craft's communications compartment.

In the upper corner of the screen two black shadows blotted on and off the surface with irregular repetition. Cap Hutch was frowning as he stared at the screen, but the expression on his florid face was considerably less worried. At last he turned to Suran and scowled. "Those can't be patrol craft," he said positively. "They're probably a couple of trading space cruisers."

Suran, the space radio officer was vastly relieved at this decision. But he asked, "What would trading cruisers be doing in this belt, Skipper? I mean, there isn't trade to amount to anything here."

Hutch shrugged.

"Off their courses, mebbe," he said. "I dunno. Could be a hundred reasons. But they don't interest me now. All I wanted to make sure about was that they wasn't patrol craft. That's certain, so what's there to worry about?"

The space radio officer scratched his head, grinned, and said he didn't know. Cap Hutch grunted and waddled out of the communications compartment. He was back again in the battle with his hangover. That was all that concerned him for the present.

In this compartment again Hutch groaned and stretched out on his bunk. He closed his eyes and fought off the demons with the skull hammers. He would have to tell Cardigan about the cruisers after a bit. They could be poachers, nosing around to drop miners on some of the outlying asteroids in the belt. They could be—

The skipper of the *Venus Maiden* fell asleep...

IT WAS late afternoon when Torgan burst excitedly in on Cardigan in the *duralloy* office shack near the space wharves. The broad-shouldered young man had been busy with engineering problems the better part of the afternoon, and looked up startledly from a disordered mess of papers.

"What's on your mind?" he asked.

"Torgan talk to stevedore, *Venus Maiden*. Stevedore say spaceships near Igakuro. Stevedore say Space Radio Boss tell Skipper Boss and rest of crew few hours back."

Cardigan's black eyebrows lifted in surprise.

"You sure of that?" he asked.

Torgan nodded.

Cardigan got up and went to the door.

"Come along," he said. "We're going to pay a visit to the *Venus Maiden*."

Cap Hutch was visibly perplexed when he was called up from the rocket room to find young Cardigan and the Igakuroan, Torgan, waiting for him on the deck of the *Venus Maiden*.

"What's the matter Cardigan?" the skipper of the tramp cargo carrier asked uneasily. "Something wrong with the supply consignments I unloaded?"

Cardigan shook his head.

"What about the spaceships your operator picked up on the *vizascreen* earlier today? Torgan heard about it from a winch hand on the wharf."

Cap Hutch snapped his fat fingers in genuine alarm.

"Damn, Cardigan," he said. "I forgot to tell you."

Cardigan stared coldly at him.

"Then tell me now, and make it quick," he said.

Hutch flushed beneath the younger man's stare, and told him in detail what he knew of the matter.

"That was several hours back?" Cardigan asked, when Hutch had concluded.

The skipper of the tramp ship nodded.

"Has your space radio officer picked them up on the screen since then?"

Hutch shook his head.

"No. He ain't been testing since then."

Cardigan turned in the direction of the communications compartment. Torgan moved along beside him.

"Come on," Cardigan snapped. "We're going to have another look at that screen."

Suran, the operator, was inside when Hutch, Cardigan, and Torgan entered. He looked up in surprise, then connected the *vizascreen* beam apparatus as Cardigan told him what he wanted. In a moment the screen was glowing pink, and Suran was twisting the dial beneath it to set the beam on the same wave at which it had been the other time.

The black outlines of two space cruisers, vastly larger than before, appeared on the screen thirty seconds later. Hutch gasped as he saw the undeniable outlines of armament on the decks of both spacecraft.

It was Cardigan who broke the startled silence.

"Trading craft, eh, Hutch?" he said, sarcastically.

"What in hell!" Hutch exclaimed whitely. "Patrol ships!"

Cardigan looked narrowly at the tramp ships skipper. "Supposing they are patrol craft, Cap? What's the reason to turn gray over that?" he demanded.

"They didn't look like patrol craft the first time," Hutch was mumbling. "They didn't at all. They didn't at all. It must be some new design they're using. For cryin' out loud!"

CARDIGAN had stepped in front of Hutch, and was staring at him in surprise. He repeated his question, and the words seemed to bring Hutch out of his momentary shock. He blinked at Cardigan, then flushed.

"You gotta help me, Cardigan!" he exclaimed. "You gotta help me! Those spaceships are coming in here—there don't seem to be no doubt about it. They'll snoop through the *Venus Maiden,* as sure as hell. They'll find the consignment."

"What consignment?"

"An unlicensed one I picked up at Venus," Hutch said redly. "I—uh—yeah, I smuggled it out. I'm supposed to carry it to Juno."

"What is it?" Cardigan asked.

"Explosive *malium,*" Hutch said, "for making atomic turbine heads. There's a hell of a tariff on the stuff. The persons who gave me the consignment order wanted to skip the tariff charges at both ports. It would save 'em a small fortune. I—uh—hell—I ain't got so much business that I can turn down a fat proposition like that. I accepted the job and packed the stuff under the hull of the *Venus Maiden.* A hundred cases of *malium.* Hell, if the patrol officers snoop and find it there and ask to see my tariff-release papers, I'll catch a fine that'll ruin me forever!"

Cardigan looked disgusted.

"Yes, and perhaps a few months in a Federation prison," he said. "But what in the hell do you think I can do to cover up for you?"

"You can get some of your natives to unload the stuff from the *Venus Maiden,*" Hutch said hoarsely, "and hide it away in one of the shack sections by the swamplands. The patrol officers won't hang around long. Then we can get the stuff back aboard the *Venus Maiden* and I'll get going."

"That's a marvelous idea, Cap," Cardigan said with heavy sarcasm. "And contains absolutely no risk to me."

Hutch's face fell and he looked miserable.

"What'll I do?" he asked.

"Maybe, if they're patrol officers, they won't snoop," Cardigan suggested. "There's no certainty that they will. It's a fifty-fifty chance, as long as you don't arouse any suspicion. Besides, I'm not thoroughly convinced that those are patrol craft."

"But they're armed, and—" Hutch began.

Cardigan nodded grimly. "I know. I can see the outlines of deck guns as clearly as you can. Nevertheless, there's no certainty that those space cruisers are part of the Interspacial Patrol. Until we know better, I don't think either of us can do much."

Cap Hutch was perplexed.

"But, Cardigan," he protested, "if they ain't part of the patrol, what are—"

Cardigan cut him off. He shrugged as he spoke.

"I'm not good at guessing. But sometimes my hunches aren't so bad."

Hutch went one shade grayer.

"Merciful mother in heaven!" he exclaimed. "You don't suppose they could be—"

Cardigan cut him off again, speaking to Torgan.

"You'd better call out your boys," he said. "Break out a case of electra-rifles and have them ready to stand by."

"Cardigan!" Hutch exclaimed in alarm.

Cardigan shrugged. "There's no sense in getting worked up, and there's no sense in jumping to conclusions," he said. "However, it's a damned good idea to be ready for anything."

CHAPTER SEVEN

IN THE oppressive damply malignant heat of the tropical swamp trails, the Reverend Zender and his daughter Carol had made far less progress in their journey than had originally been planned.

With each succeeding hour after the breaking of dawn, their halts had become more and more frequent. By noon the girl was white-faced and exhausted; her father grimly aware that he had overestimated himself.

The four Igakuroans who had accompanied them as guides and porters sat apart from the Earthman and his daughter among the equipment they carried. Their green faces were impassive, their round, red eyes unwinkingly fixed on Zender and his daughter.

"I was a fool to bring you along on this, Carol," the missionary said sickly. "I was a fool to decide to strike out for the villages on the other side of the swamps in the first place. We had only natives' word for the distance, and only their word for the existence of the village beyond there. There is nothing for us to do but swallow our pride and turn back," he concluded bitterly.

"How long has it been since we left the stockade?" the girl asked.

"Perhaps eight hours," said her father. "Perhaps a little less. It is impossible to learn from the natives how much longer the journey is. They don't seem to be able to understand what I wish to know."

"It might not be much farther," the girl said weakly. "It might be less than our return would be."

The missionary ran his big-boned hand through his hair.

"It might be," he admitted. "But if it isn't…" He let the sentence trail off.

The Reverend Zender rose. He walked over to the four impassive porters. They interpreted his action to mean a continuation of the journey, and leaped to their feet. The tall, somber-faced missionary wiped the sweat from his eyes, and shook his head. He gestured for them to sit down again. Then he pointed back in the direction from which they had come. Painfully, then, he used his knowledge of the native dialect as best he could. It seemed to him, after some three minutes of this, that they finally understood him.

Zender went back to his daughter.

"I think I made it clear that we are to rest a little longer, then start back," he said.

The girl looked at her father, and there were tears in her eyes. He seemed utterly defeated, sickly exhausted …

ON BOARD the foremost of the two black-sheened space cruisers, Malveau stood on the glassicade enclosed bridge deck. Beside him was Uska, the Junovian.

"The tramp, *Venus Maiden* lies at the far end of the wharf," Malveau was saying, "…obviously the fool of a skipper had some reason for delaying his departure."

"I wonder if it iss ssome ssort of a trap," Uska said.

Malveau looked at him sharply. "Of course not," he snapped.

"Our sspace radio operator reportss that there iss no activity on the wharfss or otherwisse," said Uska troubledly.

Malveau put scorn in his question.

"Are you afraid?"

Uska stared coldly at Malveau with his single eye. His features twisted into a grimace of anger.

"You ssay that to me?" he demanded.

"I had reason to ask," Malveau countered. "Your remarks indicated unusual concern over possible danger."

Satan came onto the bridge then, his huge body shrugging through the bulkhead entrance with little room to spare. He spoke to Uska.

"You'd better get below with the first crew, my friend," he smiled. "The mooring we make at the wharf is going to be precisely timed. We must spill from the side hatches onto the wharf with speed. The speed of our attack will be the essence of surprise."

Uska turned away, then paused. "You have taken into consideration the tramp sspaceship lying at the far end of the wharf?" he asked.

Satan nodded.

"Naturally. It is an unexpected factor, but not all that troublesome. Our second cruiser will draw alongside the tramp and blast it to fragments with atomic cannon fire. From such close range, the tramp ship will be disposed of in several minutes."

Uska nodded, relieved.

"That iss good," he said. "It troubled me."

Malveau and Satan watched the ugly, one-eyed Junovian leave the bridge. Then Satan laughed.

"The fool evidently is losing all confidence in my leadership," he said. "It troubled him—hah! More than that will trouble him very shortly."

"You have arranged for his disposal?" Malveau asked.

Satan nodded. "One of the men in his landing party is to dispose of him. Atomic pistol, in the back. Simple."

Malveau smiled thinly at this, and uneasiness returned to his eyes. Satan detected it.

"Come now, does the idea bother you?" he asked.

The thin, moustached Malveau shook his handsome head quickly—too quickly. He laughed, and the laugh was hollow.

"I was just thinking of the ease with which you win your way," he said.

"Yes," the brutish giant agreed amiably. "Yes…yes I plan everything most carefully." He suddenly had an atomic pistol in his hand. It was centered on Malveau's chest.

The expression on Malveau's face was one of sudden frozen horror. He opened his mouth to scream, but only a choked wheeze came to his trembling lips.

Satan's atomic pistol crackled in the next instant, and a searing bolt of flame crumpled Malveau's tall, thin figure like a scorched doll.

The massive brigand stared down at the hideously burned corpse of his lieutenant. He smiled, and replaced the weapon in its holster. He stepped over to the communications screen in the corner of the bridge, snapped it on.

Briefly, Satan asked the navigator at the forward controls of the cruiser how long it would be before Igakuro's wharfside was reached. He was told two hours. He snapped off the screen, stepped around Malveau's charred body, and left the bridge…

CARDIGAN had issued electra-rifles to the skipper and members of the crew of the *Venus Maiden,* ordered them from the ship, and placed them along the walls of the compound-stockade.

Torgan's native squadron, also armed with electra-rifles, had been placed by Cardigan in the swamp fringes several hundred yards from the wharfside, after stationing a two man crew from their numbers at each of the two atomic cannon concealed in the shacks on either side of the space mooring wharf. Then Cardigan joined Torgan's riflemen in the swamp fringes to wait.

The waiting had been hellish, until finally, after an hour, the faintly discernible dots in the strata had appeared. An hour more and these dots were larger. But twilight was falling, and Cardigan sensed that the approaching cruisers were moving in now at half-speed in order to make certain of arriving in darkness.

Cardigan no longer considered the possibility that the approaching space cruisers were patrol craft. And now the waiting was charged with a new excitement, as Cardigan sent a native runner into the swampland with a message for Bennett.

Another hour passed, and Igakuro was blanketed in blackness. The throbbing of the rocket motors of the approaching cruisers was now faintly audible, and for another ten minutes grew increasingly more distinct. Then the sound was cut off, and Cardigan sensed that the cruisers were moving in with atomic mooring motors.

Hutch arrived from the stockade compound. He came stealthily through the swamp brush to Cardigan's side.

"The men along the stockade walls are getting out of hand," he whispered huskily. "What in the hell can I tell 'em?"

"Tell them to carry out orders," Cardigan said quietly, "unless they want to die quickly. You realize, of course, that those aren't patrol craft coming in?" he added sarcastically.

Hutch nodded, mopping his brow with a crumpled handkerchief.

"Hell yes, and so do the men. But what're we expected to do?"

"Hold fire until we break from this swamp fringe and make for the stockade. Then open up to cover our retreat. Tell them to keep their fire high and well over our heads. When we get to the stockade, I'll take over."

The skipper of the tramp ship left, and Cardigan went forward to have a hurried consultation with each of the gun crews on either side of the mooring wharf. He instructed them to hold fire until the cruisers were actually moored. Then he returned to Torgan's riflemen at the swamp edge.

It happened with incredible swiftness just five minutes later.

Torgan saw the black hulls of the space cruisers before Cardigan did. He grabbed Cardigan's arm excitedly, pointing wordlessly. And then Cardigan saw them.

ONE of the cruisers was leading the other—it seemed for a moment. Then, abruptly, the rear cruiser was swinging up parallel to the *Venus Maiden* into a range less than twenty yards off, while the other slid silently to motor mooring at the other end of the wharfside.

The gun crew at the atomic cannon concealed in the shack to the left of the wharf opened fire, the flash of flame spitting toward the cruiser at mooring.

There was a sudden wild whoop from a dozen throats, and men were tumbling from the side hatches of the moored cruiser to the wharf. A blasting bolt of crimson from the gun deck of that cruiser answered the atomic cannon in the right shack an instant later, and flame leaped high with explosive brilliance as the right shack burst into fragments.

Cardigan gave the order to Torgan, and the native guards opened fire at the running figures on the dock, using the momentary glare from the demolished shack to sight their human targets.

Electra-rifles snapped back their answer, and the cannon on the deck of the motor moored cruiser sent a blast of crimson flame flashing into the stockade-compound. The explosion there was terrific.

Cardigan was cursing, demanding profanely to know why the gun crew in the left shack hadn't opened fire. And then he saw the fleeing figures in the darkness—figures dashing from the shack toward the comparative safety of the swamp brush. His face went rigid with rage at the realization that the native gun crew had deserted the atomic cannon in terror without firing a shot.

Cardigan put his own electra-rifle to his shoulder, aimed carefully, and fired. The foremost of the panic stricken deserters flopped forward several yards from the swamp fringe. Cardigan fired again, and the second native toppled over dead.

Cardigan turned back to the battle, and saw that several of the attackers already lay dead on the wharf from the accurate fire of Torgan's Igakuroan crew. The others had taken shelter behind bales, packing cases, and pilings, and were keeping up a steady answering fire at Cardigan's position.

The second cruiser, the one that had run up parallel to the *Venus Maiden,* opened fire then. And Cardigan saw its purpose instantly as the first shot from that craft smashed explosively into the tramp ship's stern. The *Venus Maiden* was to be decimated, and thus block any possible retreat in her.

The cruiser stood off and sent a second atomic cannon blast into the side of the *Venus Maiden* slightly forward of amidships. And in the next instant the planet rocked to the incredible explosion that shook the wharfside and bathed the entire landscape in a sheet of flame.

Cardigan was thrown forward on his face through the terrific concussion of the blast. He picked himself up, ears ringing, nose bleeding, while the ground still trembled beneath him.

The wharf near where the *Venus Maiden* had been moored was nothing but a twisted scar of molten *duralloy.* The tramp ship and the cruiser, which had fired on her from a range of twenty yards, were nowhere to be seen.

And suddenly Cardigan was laughing almost hysterically in the realization of what had happened. The brigand cruiser had fired into the hold compartments where Hutch's smuggled cases of highly explosive *malium* had been stored. The resultant blast had utterly destroyed both the *Venus Maiden* and her attacker.

CARDIGAN looked for the first cruiser that had moored at the other end of the wharf, wildly hoping that it had suffered some damage from the blast; but then the deck gun of that craft opened fire again with furious rapidity, sending bolt upon bolt of flame blasting into the stockade-compound.

The thunderous explosions behind him told him of the devastating bombardment Hutch and his crew were receiving. And the futile hysteria of answering electra-rifle fire told him of the panic of its defenders. Cardigan turned to Torgan and shouted the order for withdrawal to the stockade.

There were but half a dozen native riflemen left of Torgan's original squad of twenty, even though only five lay dead in the swamp bushes. Cardigan realized that the others had fled in the confusion of the battle, and he cursed them futilely as he and Torgan rallied the remnants of the band for the retreat to the compounds.

The individual fire from the attackers on the wharf had ceased completely, but the cruiser's deck gun continued to blast explosive blots of flame unerringly into the stockade.

Cardigan and Torgan had nursed the half dozen native riflemen through several hundred yards of swamp brush and were still a hundred yards from the compounds when it became apparent that their objective was no longer suitable for either shelter or defense.

The stockade-compound was an inferno of flame, torch-lighting the terrain around it for more than a hundred yards. All sign of resistance from it had ceased, and Cardigan was sickly certain that Hutch and the dozen or more members of his crew had perished in the brutal bombardment.

Cardigan turned wordlessly to the massive Torgan. The huge Igakuroan was staring dumbly at the blazing ruins of the stockade, the flames from which were already spreading to the native village just outside it.

The bombardment suddenly ceased and, save for wild shouting from the attackers on the wharfside, the only sound was the crackling of the blazing settlement.

Torgan's mouth was taut, his face rigid. He tore his eyes from the blazing ruins and looked at Cardigan.

"They be here soon," the huge native said slowly. "We move hell out of here quick." He pointed into the swampy jungles.

Cardigan nodded, and turned away to follow Torgan into the thick, enveloping blackness of the tangled swampland. The rest of the native riflemen had deserted, but neither Cardigan nor his faithful native companion gave any sign of knowing it. Behind them the yells of the triumphant brigands grew faint, swallowed in the oppressive curtain of jungle blackness.

Soon there was no sound except that of their own legs slogging knee-deep through the treacherous marshes of the swamp wastes...

CHAPTER EIGHT

BENNETT had started back immediately when the message carried by the frightened native runner arrived. There had been no time for him to rally any of the natives in the mines, and the effort would have been useless since there were no weapons in the *vardium* fields with which to arm them. He was aware, also, that the native miners, on hearing the tale of impending attack from the messenger who had brought Cardigan's note to him, would undoubtedly take to the jungle for safety and hiding until the trouble was over. But trying to prevent such a reaction, he knew, would also be futile.

There was nothing for him to do, Bennett knew, save continue toward the compound-stockade alone and as swiftly as possible. En route, he could at least prepare plans to cover several possibilities he might encounter when he got there.

Bennett had left all heavy equipment, save his electra-rifle and atomic pistols, behind him when he'd started back, and was consequently able to make excellent time through the tangled underbrush of the short-cut he had selected.

He ran with a loping, easy gait that ate up distance, and slowed to a walk each quarter of an hour to refurbish his strength. He had proceeded this way less than two hours when the sounds of battle finally came to his ears. As he struggled onward, he was soon able to recognize the explosive shriek of atomic cannonading, and tell, further, that it was not the sound made by the obsolete atomic guns that he and Cardigan had mounted for protection on the wharf-side.

The sickening explanation for this was instantly apparent to Bennett. Their own atomic cannon was either unmanned or put out of action. The other atomic cannon was that of the raiding party. The situation was consequently highly unfavorable.

Bennett's loose stride was jerky, stumbling, now, and his lean young face blackened with grime and streaming sweat. Each breath was as a burning sob in his lungs; and a creeper vine sent him spilling forward to the thick slime of the marshland a few moments later.

As Bennett struggled to his feet and started forward again, the stabbing fire of pain in his left ankle brought an involuntary groan from his lips. He hobbled to a stop, forcing himself to pause long enough to wrest the thick boot from his foot.

A glance at the rapidly swelling bruise below his ankle told him, more than the pain itself, that the sprain was particularly bad. He gritted his teeth, and forced his heavy boot back over the foot, the pain of the effort lancing brutally through his weary body.

Bennett made two efforts to continue forward. The first sent him sprawling to the slime again the moment he threw his weight upon his bad ankle.

He picked himself up, unslung his electra-rifle and tried to use it as a crutch. The butt of the weapon sank suckingly into the slime, slipping swiftly forward and pitching Bennett over on his side.

IT WAS then that the thundering reverberation of the blast from the wharfside shook the ground beneath Bennett, stunning him momentarily, deafening his eardrums, and shaking the planet with earthquaking violence.

Dazedly, Bennett lifted himself to one elbow, shaking his head to clear his stunned senses of sight and hearing. He inched forward until his groping hand found his electra-rifle, then, using the weapon as a staff, he pulled himself to a sitting position, and tried again to rise.

The effort this time was more successful, though it drenched his already soaked body with a cold wave of sweat. He stood there, teetering against the electra-rifle's support, gathering strength enough to continue.

Then he started forward again, slowly, painfully, hobbling in a lurching sort of seesaw.

Ten yards further Bennett stumbled and pitched forward to the slime again. He lay motionless for perhaps a minute, then began the exhausting ritual of rising once more. The atomic cannonading from the wharfside was still uninterrupted, the sporadic electra-rifle fire blending dimly into the background.

Voices were faint in Bennett's ears, now. Voices blurring into the background of battle. He struggled slowly forward again, and five yards further on, fell once more.

Bennett heard the voices more clearly, now, and the crashing of bodies through the underbrush. He raised his head, turning himself on his side as he did so, sliding his elbow beneath his body to form a bridge for the electra-rifle which he slowly brought to a firing position. The angry noises of battle continued, as did the crashing sounds in the underbrush and the approach of voices.

Bennett clenched his teeth, blinking away the sweat and pain that blurred his vision, peering grimly along the sights of his electra-rifle as he trained it on the spot in the underbrush ahead from which the sound of approaching voices was loudest.

He waited, the sweat rolling over his face in cold waves. Waited, as he tried to concentrate his dazed and weary mind upon the sound of the voices against the confusing sound pattern of the battle.

Bennett saw the underbrush move, then. Move directly before the sights of his weapon. His thumb went taut against the firing button, the pressure a scant hair-weight from that required to send an electra-bolt flashing directly into the moving brush.

He was almost able to discern the shadowy bulk of the person crashing through the brush toward him, and grimly decided to hold his fire only long enough for a split-second identification of the approaching bush-prowler.

If it were Cardigan, or some loyal Igakuroan, or even old Hutch, such split-second recognition would be simple. But should it be otherwise, Bennett determined to shoot first and identify at leisure.

Now the voices had stopped abruptly.

The brush was parting...

THE firing had ceased by his order, and now Satan stood on the shattered wharfside of Igakuro, grimly surveying the cost of his raid.

The explosion of the other cruiser had been a catastrophic shock to the massive Earth renegade. It had been an integral factor in the completion of his sacking of the planet. But he had pushed the disaster temporarily from his mind, inasmuch as there had been the attack to carry out.

Uska had been slain as Satan had ordered, by an atomic pistol blast from behind as the lieutenant led the first wave of the raiders onto the docks. The dark, lean, effeminate Earthman had been eliminated by Satan himself. Uska had been dispatched by Jekka. Each of these slayings according to plans conceived before the disaster to the second cruiser occurred.

Satan's renegade navigator-skipper had been one of those who perished in the explosion of the second craft. And Satan had never intended to dispatch that necessary lieutenant to his plans.

Polo had gathered the brigands together in the shattered wharf by the massive leader's order, once the firing had ceased. And there were now scarcely more than a dozen of them left.

Satan moved along the space mooring dock wordlessly, identifying those who had been slain by the electra-rifles of Igakuro's futile defenders. Then he returned to the Junovian, Polo, and ordered him to place two men on watch aboard the remaining cruiser, sending the rest forward to occupy the ruins of the compound-stockade.

"We will remain until dawn," Satan told his stocky lieutenant. "And then we shall hunt the *var-dust* caches underground. The loss of our sister ship makes it impossible to plan on waiting here for any further supply of the alloy to be wrested from the mines. We have but one vessel on which to carry what we can seize. Our plans have consequently been considerably altered."

Polo nodded, turned and bellowed instructions to the dozen or so brigands who waited patiently on the dock. Two returned to take watch aboard the black-sheened cruiser, and the remainder moved slowly for the ruins of the compound-stockade.

"What of continued resistance?" Polo demanded. "Do you think we will find any more?"

"I can tell you that," Satan said, "when we count corpses in the compound-stockade and along the underbrush fringe from which their principle electra-rifle fire came."

Satan shrugged, his dark features glowering.

"Until then," he added, "we must wait." His voice was ragged, angry. He started out for the ruins of the stockade compound, his thug lieutenant following along behind him.

It was fully a dozen minutes later when Polo and Satan finished their inspection of the dead in the stockade-compound.

"There are enough to fully account for the crew aboard the space tramper," Polo said quietly. "We can be certain they are all eliminated."

Satan shrugged his massive shoulders, staring down at a body crumpled beside his feet.

"Perhaps," he said. "But there was none among these dead who could have been Bennett or Cardigan."

"We have yet to inspect the underbrush fringe from which the electra-rifle fire came," Polo put in.

Satan glowered, prodding the body with his foot. There was a faint moan, and the massive brigand leader's eyes flashed to meet Polo's then back to the body.

"This one survived, it seems," Satan said.

The faint moan was repeated.

Satan pulled an atomic pistol from his hip-holster. He turned the body with his foot, rolling it over face upward.

The badly burned features that looked sightlessly up at Satan and his lieutenant were those of Cap Hutch. The burned, puffed lips parted and another faint moan escaped them.

Satan trained his atomic pistol on the wounded space tramp skipper's head. He fired once, unerringly, and what was left of Hutch stirred and groaned no longer.

Satan turned to Polo.

"Come," he snapped irritably, shoving the weapon back into its holster. "We must search for the bodies of Cardigan and Bennett."

THE Reverend Zender and his daughter were several hours from their return to the compound-stockade when the noises of the sudden battle reached their ears.

The missionary had been at the fore of their tiny safari, directly behind the lead guide. For part of the journey he had carried his exhausted daughter in his arms, and for much of it she had been able to walk along the slimy mire of the trail beside him with just the assistance of his arm.

The front Igakuroan guide heard the gunfire before either the missionary or his daughter did. His abrupt halt and frightened face, therefore, were puzzling to Zender and his daughter, Carol.

It was only when the native bolted, dashing back along the line of porters and screaming wild gibberish at them, that the opening cannonading reached the ears of the two Earth people.

And before either of them could adjust themselves to the swift purpose of their guides, the Igakuroans had fled into the thick concealment of the underbrush.

That was the last that Reverend Zender or his daughter Carol saw of their guides. Their equipment was dumped crazily into the short brush and thick slime of the trail, and the Igakuroans had vanished but seconds later.

The gaunt, somber-visaged missionary stared wordlessly, grimly, in the direction of the battle sounds, his daughter holding tightly to his arm.

Finally he turned to her.

His face was bleak, washed of all emotion save the pity that shone from his eyes for the girl.

"Carol," he began. Suddenly he choked, impulsively placing his big, gnarled hands on her shoulders. "You know what this—this means?"

Carol made a brave attempt to hide her fear. Her white teeth bit into her full underlip and she smiled tremulously, shaking her head.

"It is a brigand raid of some sort," the missionary said quietly. "There could be no other explanation. It is not a native revolt, otherwise our Igakuroan guides would have turned on us instead of fleeing."

"What are we to do?" the girl asked.

The tall, gaunt Zender hesitated for just a moment.

"You are not afraid, Carol?"

"No," the girl answered.

He took his hands from her shoulders.

"Then there is only one thing for us to do," he declared quietly. "We must continue with all haste to the stockade-compound. Cardigan and Bennett will need whatever assistance we can give them."

"Yes, Father," Carol Zender said. "It is the only thing for us to do."

The tall missionary turned, surveying the trail ahead. He spoke as if to himself, though his words were addressed to the girl.

"If there was some place of safety for you," he said huskily, "I would leave you there. However, we do not know if the brigands have landed at other points on the planet, and it is more certain to find safety for you inside the stockade."

"But…but without the Igakuroan guides," the girl began, "we—"

Her father cut her off.

"I realize," he admitted, "that we will have difficulty in finding our way through the trail tangles back to the compound-stockade. However, we must attempt it. I shall do my best."

The girl nodded, and her father slipped his arm about her slim shoulders, giving her needed support as they set off slowly along the swampy marsh-line of the trail…

CHAPTER NINE

CARDIGAN and the huge Igakuroan, Torgan, reached Vardium Shaft Eighty shortly before dawn broke on the tiny planet. The short, wide-shouldered young Earthman and the massive native were each comparatively fresh, although the short-cut course through some of the most treacherous swampland on the planet had been especially arduous.

Cardigan glanced around the deserted drill shacks, the empty shaft workings, and looked bitterly at Torgan.

"They all got the hell away in a hurry," he observed. "I don't imagine an Igakuroan skull will poke out of the swamp jungle brush for another year."

Torgan shuffled his big, naked feet uncomfortably and looked away. The bitterness left Cardigan's mouth, and he touched the native's hugely muscled forearm apologetically.

"It's all right. I don't suppose I can blame them. It isn't their fight. Your sticking by me makes up for as much as your comrades-under-the-green-skin could have done."

"Bennett Boss come back here?" Torgan asked.

Cardigan nodded, frowning.

"I hope to hell he does. He should have sense enough to realize what's happened to the resistance we offered on the wharfside and from the stockade, once he gets within reconnaissance range of things. The message I sent him should have reached him shortly before the fight opened up. His departure from here would bring him almost half the distance back to the stockade before the mess stopped. That would give him time, however, to be here waiting to rendezvous with us by now."

"Bennett Boss maybe not turn back for here," Torgan suggested.

Cardigan shrugged. "Perhaps not. But he'd realize, of course, that any brigand raid would be directed at our *var-dust* supply, and inasmuch as the *var-dust* is cached underground only a few hundred yards off the trail, here, he'd know that any retreat we'd make would be to protect it."

"Bennett Boss see maybe all dead. Think maybe you dead. Maybe take cover other side planet," Torgan said.

Cardigan said nothing to this. He walked over to the shaft edge and sat down wearily, unslinging his electra-rifle and dropping it to his lap.

Torgan turned and went off down the trail a few yards. He stood there motionless, facing the direction of the stockades. Cardigan watched the massive native expressionlessly. After several minutes, Torgan turned and came back to Cardigan.

"No follow us. No person on trail," he said.

Cardigan nodded in satisfaction. "That's some consolation. They probably don't realize as yet that anyone came out from under their attack alive. They'll probably put a check on their start for the *var-dust* cache until they can count heads and reorganize. The blow-up of the extra cruiser was obviously not in their plans. I figure they'll get under way from the stockade—or what's left of it—sometime around dawn."

TORGAN nodded solemnly at what he digested of Cardigan's summation.

"Then what we do, Cardigan Boss?" he asked.

Cardigan looked up sharply at the huge native. A flicker of a grin touched his mouth.

"You can ask the damnedest questions, Torgan," he said.

Torgan nodded agreeably to the statement.

"Maybe Cardigan Boss think I take post down trail, keep watch," the Igakuroan said.

"A good idea," Cardigan agreed. "Mile, half mile, down main trail. Keep look-out."

Torgan nodded and turned away, moving swiftly down the trail in the direction of the stockade. His huge green-skinned body was lost from sight in the thick tangle of the verdant undergrowth a few minutes later.

Cardigan rose, carrying his electra-rifle under his arm, and began to pace nervously back and forth before the deserted mine shaft.

"Damn him," he muttered anxiously. "What's happened to him?"

After five more minutes of this irritable panthering back and forth, Cardigan returned to the shaft side and sat down again. He remained in this position for several minutes, then rose abruptly.

"Dammit!" he snapped explosively. "This waiting has gone on too long. Something's happened to Pete! Maybe those devils have done him in!"

Cardigan slung his electra-rifle over his shoulder and began a swift, swinging trot along the trail in the direction Torgan had taken. A moment later and he was beating aside the overhanging tangle of swamp vegetation that marked the entrance of the tunnel-like trail. Five minutes after that, still swinging along at his swift, loose pace, he came upon Torgan.

The huge native stepped out from the concealment of brush beside the trail.

"Something wrong, Cardigan Boss?"

Cardigan said, "Bennett Boss. Too long overdue. Must find, Torgan. What short cut would he take in hell of a hurry?"

Torgan thought a moment.

"We go back shaft," he said.

Cardigan nodded, and let the huge Igakuroan lead him as they started back to the shaft. When they were back in the drill clearings and at the shaft again, Torgan surveyed the scene.

Cardigan waited patiently, while the swamp-wise Igakuroan searched for some sign of the short cut on which Bennett had started. Several minutes passed.

At last, stopping before a small gap-tunnel leading into the underbrush at the edge of the clearing, Torgan turned to Cardigan.

"Think maybe Bennett Boss start here," the massive native said.

"Let's get going," Cardigan said.

Torgan grunted something in his own tongue and shouldered into the inky opening at the edge of the clearing. The saffron of Igakuroan dawn was slanting into the sky over the clearing as the two entered the thick tangle of the swamp jungle again. In a moment the dawn was replaced by the blackness of the *astera-tropical* jungle around them.

THROUGH the thick slime of the marshland underfooting, Cardigan followed the guidance of the massive Igakuroan doggedly. The massive native moved with the easy certainty of one born to swamp lore, seemingly able to pierce the blackness with a vision that was beacon-like.

Now and again Torgan stopped, inspecting a print, or a telltale fragment of thread on a thorn-crusted creeper vine. Cardigan grimly marveled at the native's certainty in inspecting each of these signs, but was breathlessly relieved every time another tell-tale mark further along gave assurance that the last clue had not been misread.

Several times Cardigan slipped forward in the stinking slime of a marsh, only to climb cursing to his feet, while the massive native waited patiently. Then they would be off again, Torgan leading the way with a swift, tireless stride that knew no uncertainty.

Only after an hour passed did Torgan halt, insisting that Cardigan spend several minutes regaining his strength and bringing the wind back to his aching lungs. Cardigan cursed the native, then, insisting that he was still able to continue. But after the short rest, he realized the soundness of his guide's decision when they were able to proceed again with considerably more speed.

Half an hour further on, Torgan halted, turning to Cardigan, pointing to an indistinct smear across the gray-black slime of the marshland mud.

Cardigan looked questioningly at Torgan.

"What does it mean?"

"Bennett Boss, not far ahead," Torgan said.

"Thank God!" Cardigan gasped.

The undergrowth was thicker, the tangler and creeper vines much more treacherous as Cardigan started on behind the hulking frame of the huge Igakuroan.

Torgan used his huge body and his electra-rifle as both wedge and scythe to clear the way for Cardigan following him. Cardigan was cursing jubilantly, now, in a relief that was almost hysterical. Torgan accompanied this with pleased grunts and gabblings of pride.

Less than three minutes later Torgan slashed through the brush and out into a small clearing, Cardigan directly on his heels.

It was Torgan who grunted, "Bennett Boss!"

And then Cardigan saw his partner. Bennett was lying at the other edge of the tiny clearing, propped up on one elbow, electra-rifle grasped tightly in white-knuckled hands, pointed unwaveringly at them!

"Pete!" Cardigan cried out.

The electra-rifle wavered, then the barrel of the weapon nosed forward and the rifle slid from Bennett's hands.

"You dope!" Bennett gasped, a sickly grin forcing the corners of his mouth up momentarily. Then, face ashen, his head dropped forward into the black-gray ooze of marsh slime.

Torgan was across the tiny clearing in an instant, Cardigan several paces behind. The huge Igakuroan bent over and lifted the lean, wiry body of Cardigan's partner into his arms in a gentle effortless gesture. He turned to face Cardigan.

"We go back?"

Cardigan nodded.

"Right, old blood-hound!" he grinned. He stepped over and picked up the electra-rifle that had fallen from Bennett's grasp when he'd fainted. He slung this over his shoulder beside his own and followed Torgan back across the tiny clearing the way they had come. Torgan paused at the edge of the clearing.

"Quick way Bennett Boss pick not damn quick enough for Torgan," he said.

"You know a shorter way?" Cardigan demanded.

Torgan nodded. "Shorter. Harder. Take?"

"Take," said Cardigan...

AS THE Reverend Zender and his daughter, Carol, made their way laboriously back through the oppressive blackness of the swamp jungles, the sounds of conflict came increasingly, ominously, louder to their ears.

Zender had used these sounds of battle to guide their progress, however, and through them managed to regain bearings when the swamp marsh tangle seemed to thwart them utterly.

The occasions on which the two were forced to pause for rest were numerous; for the girl, though grimly determined not to falter, found the strain of the battle against the *astera-tropical* jungle increasingly more exhausting.

In spite of this, however, their progress was swift, and they soon found themselves at a trail fork that was at last recognizable to the tall, gaunt missionary.

Almost simultaneous with their discovery of this familiar trail fork, the sounds of battle ceased abruptly.

The missionary had demanded that his daughter rest a few moments once more, and they were seated at the side of the fork when the eerie strangeness of the sudden battle lull became at once apparent to them both.

The sharp glance of alarm that Carol gave her father was anxiously questioning.

"They've stopped," she said. "What does that mea—"

The Reverend Zender answered his daughter's question before it was completed.

"It might perhaps signify a lull of but a few moments," he said gravely. "Or it might mean that the battle is done." His expression was wooden. "We should learn which it is within a few more minutes," he added.

The girl nodded wordlessly, her eyes filled with sudden fear.

The minutes passed, while the ominous silence held. Zender wiped the perspiration from his gaunt face, glancing at his daughter. He rose, then, abruptly.

"I think it best that we continue on, Carol," he said. "The battle, I am almost certain, has come to an end." He ran a big hand through the matted tangle of his lank dark hair, and his wide, thin-lipped mouth went tight in determination.

The girl rose instantly.

"If the fight is over," she began, "do you suppose that—"

Her father cut off her question.

"It is impossible to tell who has been the victor, Carol. We will have no way of knowing until we arrive at the compound-stockade. Then—" He broke off.

"If the others have won?" the girl asked.

"We must do what we can," Zender answered. "But until we arrive, there is no certainty of that."

"Father," Carol said swiftly, "you don't intend to—" She was unable to finish the question.

"I must do all that I can," the missionary answered simply.

"But you are unarmed!" the girl protested. "If the brigands have won the stockade, and the wharf is in their hands, there is nothing you could do, Father. If Bennett and Cardigan and their native guards were unable to beat off the attack, surely it is madness for you to think that you could succeed where they have failed!"

"I said merely that I will do what I am able," the missionary declared. "And I repeat, we cannot tell what lies ahead until we come to it."

They started off along the trail again, and the silence was more ominous than the noise of battle had been before.

It was scarcely half an hour later when they heard the first of the brigand voices, and caught the first flickerings of flame from the stockade dimly ahead in the blackness.

Save for a short, swift tension in his arm around Carol's shoulder, Zender did not betray an emotional response to this. They continued onward for another quarter of a mile, at which point the missionary wordlessly guided his daughter into the thick fringes of the jungle trail.

"Our concealment will be more simple, should any of them be coming in this direction," he explained.

IT was considerably later when the missionary and his daughter at last arrived at the edge of the jungle clearing in which lay the ruined huts of what had been the Igakuroan village just beyond the compound stockade.

The scene before them was one of charred devastation, utter destruction. Not a hut in the village had been spared by what had obviously been swiftly speeding flame.

The girl remained in the clearing fringes, while Zender went stealthily forward to investigate. When he returned some fifteen minutes later his mouth was a tight, hard line of cold anger.

"The natives managed to flee to the jungles," he reported. "There was no trace of any of their—their bodies in the ashes of the village ruins. The stockade beyond, however," and he paused, his great fists working in rage, "is a scene of carnage. All of the crew from the *Venus Maiden* seem to have been slaughtered while defending the stockade walls. The brigands are in what's left of the compound buildings. They've evidently posted several men aboard their raiding cruiser off the wharf."

The girl listened to her father with white-faced horror, her lips compressed into a thin line of anger. As he paused, she interrupted him quietly.

"What do you imagine they plan next, Father?"

"The *var-dust* deposits cached away in Cardigan and Bennett's underground vaults are undoubtedly what they're after," he said. "I was able to overhear two sentries mentioning the underground vault. The plan is to start for there at dawn."

"And where is the vault located?"

"In the vicinity of Shaft Eighty," the missionary said. "Young Bennett mentioned it to me the evening of our arrival."

There was a silence. Carol Zender finally broke it.

"And what do you plan to do, Father?"

"I'm not sure, yet," he declared. "Just now there is nothing to do. You must rest. If we withdraw a little more into the jungle we will be safe temporarily. I'll stand guard while you sleep, and I shall be able to rest somewhat myself."

The girl rose, her face suddenly calm. "Very well, Father," she said...

THE missionary woke his daughter shortly before the Igakuroan dawn broke. As the girl sleepily opened her eyes, she saw the electra-rifle that her father carried in the crook of his arm, and her face was suddenly startledly anxious.

"I found this beside the body of an Igakuroan guard," Zender explained. "Evidently the brigands did not get around to looting all the dead."

It was then that Carol became aware of the voices in the distance. She turned her head sharply in the direction from which they came—the direction of the stockade-compound and the desolated native village.

"They are awake and preparing to start for Shaft Eighty," the missionary said. "I am not certain but I believe they number ten at the most, not including those two left aboard their space cruiser. We will wait until they are on their way."

"Then?" the girl asked.

"Then to the cruiser," Zender said. "I don't believe the guards left aboard will remain awake once their comrades start into the jungle. From a hiding place near the wharfside I heard them bemoaning the fact that they were forced to go sleepless while their companions rested."

The voices coming from the stockade-compound suddenly became less audible, dwindling slowly until they ceased entirely.

The missionary and his daughter exchanged glances.

"They are getting under way," Zender declared. "Wait here."

The girl shook her head.

"No, Father. I'm going with you. There are two aboard that cruiser."

The Reverend Zender stared wordlessly at the girl a moment, then answered. "I am not going to the cruiser until I am certain the others are on their way," he said. "Please remain here, Carol, until I return."

The girl started to object, then bit her underlip and said nothing.

"Will you promise to remain here?" her father asked.

Silently, the girl nodded.

The missionary stepped forward and touched the girl's shoulder briefly, wordlessly, his eyes speaking his emotions.

The silence held for several moments. Then he said, "Good girl."

He turned away then, and strode into the thick green tangle of the undergrowth. The girl watched her father disappear into the verdant jungle wall, then waited until the sound of his body crashing through the brush was dim in the distance.

Then she set out after him.

THE missionary watched the brigands pass along the trail a scant fifty yards from where he crouched in the concealment of the jungle brush. He held his electra-rifle in his hands, his knuckles going white as his fingers tightened on the stock.

When the last of the small procession had passed, Zender stepped out onto the trail and started back in the direction from which they had come. It was many minutes later when the gaunt, grim figure of the missionary stepped back into the concealment of the green swamp jungles, striking through the brush to bring himself to the edge of the clearing near the space-mooring wharf.

There he crouched and watched, scarcely breathing, his eyes steadily regarding the black-sheened space cruiser moored at the extreme end of the wharf.

Satisfied at last that he saw no signs of life, Zender emerged from his concealment and moved swiftly across the clearing toward the space cruiser. He ran low, bent well forward, his tall frame silhouetted grotesquely against the gray murkiness of dawn.

He reached the wharf unchallenged, and gained the side of the big cruiser split-seconds later, moving swiftly toward the disembarkation hatch that yawned blackly open a scant twenty yards on.

There was no sign there of the two sentries who had guarded the cruiser from that post several hours before. Silently, Zender moved up the sloping gang-walk into the side-hatch opening. He almost stumbled over a dozing guard sprawled there.

The fellow snorted, spluttered, and started to cry out. In swift and vicious repetition the missionary brought his electra-rifle butt smashing down on his skull again and again. The guard was no longer breathing when Zender bent over his body moments later.

The missionary had scarcely turned away from his victim when he heard the puzzled shout of the other guard ring through the darkness. The voice came from a compartment at the end of the corridor onto which the side-hatch had opened. The sharp query was in Venusian.

The missionary shouted back instantly, in the same tongue, and was rewarded by the sound of a door slamming and feet running down the corridor toward the side-hatch opening.

Zender stepped back and waited.

He reappeared just as the second guard stumbled upon the body of his comrade in the darkness. Reappeared and swung the weapon in his hand, club-fashion, against the back of the Venusian brigand's neck. The sound of snapping bone was sharp and satisfying, and the brigand grunted and toppled forward across the body of his comrade.

The missionary waited, not daring to breathe, listening intently. There might have been a change. There might be more than two. A minute passed, and the silence held. There were no others. The Reverend Zender expelled his breath heavily, and leaned back against the side-hatch.

He stared at the bodies in the darkness at his feet, and suddenly realized that he was trembling from head to foot. He looked at the rifle in his hands, horror and disgust flooding him as his big fingers touched the sticky stock. Sickly, he let it drop to the floor.

The Reverend Zender drew in a deep, shuddering breath and fought off the nausea that momentarily assailed him. His wide, thin-lipped mouth went taut, and he straightened his shoulders.

He looked around for another weapon, and saw the small pouch lying near the hatch opening. The bulge of the small, round objects in the pouch told him what it contained. He stepped over to it and picked it up...

The Reverend Zender found Carol lying beside the trail when he started back from the cruiser some ten minutes later. The girl was unconscious, and a purple bruise marked her forehead. The rock against which she had fallen was less than a foot from her head, and the thorny crawler-vine that had tripped her was in evidence.

He, stared at her for a moment of horror, then bent and lifted her into his arms. She was breathing softly, but regularly, and her heartbeat was strong.

The missionary looked around him in despair. There was no place he could safely leave her, and no time in which to bring her back to consciousness. He made his decision without further hesitation, and started down the trail in the direction the brigands had taken, his daughter still in his arms...

TORGAN'S ROUTE proved to be incredibly more difficult and treacherous than the one over which the giant Igakuroan and the rugged Cardigan had tracked down Bennett. But as the green-skinned guide had promised, it was considerably more direct.

The trio arrived—at Shaft Eighty in but half the time the outward leg of the journey had taken. The bright heat of early Igakuroan morning had supplanted the saffron shafts of dawn, which had lighted the wide drill clearing when they had first set out from it.

Although in his time estimate on the potential movements of the brigands Cardigan had predicted that they would wait until dawn to start out for the *var-dust* loot, he took no chances on his calculations being overly optimistic. He sent Torgan back along the main trail to guard against any premature approach of the brigands, while he went to work on Bennett's ankle with supplies from the medicine kits he took from the drill shaft shacks.

Bennett had regained consciousness, and through his partner's ministrations of strong restoratives, was clear-headed and considerably less exhausted than when they'd found him in the swamp jungles.

At Bennett's insistence, Cardigan had permitted his partner to try to walk. But the effort had been futile, and brought a fresh wave of nausea and dizzying pain to Bennett.

The blond young engineer sat weakly back, biting his underlip as tears came to his eyes.

"Dammit, Cleve," he cursed, "I'm a drag, not a help. You should shoot me, and travel light."

Cardigan snapped his fingers.

"That's a hell of a fine idea," he exclaimed.

Bennett looked at him somewhat startledly, as Cardigan turned away, dashed into a drill shack, and returned again a few moments later with a small box in his hand.

"Off with that space boot again," Cardigan said. He removed the boot from Bennett's injured foot as the other gritted his teeth against the pain.

Then Cardigan busily began to unwind the bandage wrappings he had so painstakingly put on his partner's horribly swollen ankle moments before.

Bennett watched hopefully, as Cardigan opened the small box he'd taken from the drill shack. Cardigan brought forth a hypo needle and a small glass tube, which he inserted in it.

He looked up at Bennett and grinned.

"We're going to shoot your leg," he said. "Full of *novophene*. Strictly local anesthetic. It'll leave you your reflex control and sensation in that foot without any further pain. I'll slap the brace wrappings back on the foot once it's full of the stuff. That'll prevent any motion of it that might be permanently injurious. In ten minutes you'll be able to put that foot under a drill driver without a touch of pain."

Bennett's grin was broad and appreciative.

"You're a conniving cutthroat," he said. "Any medical society would oust you for a stunt like that. But go ahead, butcher. I love it."

Cardigan drove the needle into Bennett's ankle.

"What the hell," he said. "No one can snatch my medical license. I haven't got one."

AS Cardigan had predicted, Bennett was able to move around on his feet again in ten minutes, even though he hobbled slightly. Torgan came back to the clearing as Bennett was slapping his partner's back.

"They on way along trail!"

The grin left Cardigan's face. "How far away?" he asked.

"They no know trail. Move damn slow," Torgan said, frowning in calculation. "They mile and half away now, closer two mile. Take maybe half hour, maybe little more half hour."

Bennett broke in.

"How many come?" he demanded.

"All many," said Torgan, holding up both hands, fingers spread.

"Ten, eh?" Cardigan frowned. "And we're three," he added thoughtfully. He turned to Bennett, still frowning. "If we're gonna save our hides and our fortune, Pete," he said, "we'll have to think fast. Any ideas?"

"Trail ambush," Bennett suggested after a moment.

"We're only three," Cardigan said, shaking his head. "We'd have damn little chance for that."

Bennett nodded in agreement.

"You're right," he admitted. "It was just the first thing that popped into my skull."

"Blow up once," Torgan said regretfully, referring to the explosion caused by the *Venus Maiden*—which had destroyed the second of the raiding space cruisers. "Too bad no chance blow up again." He shrugged his big shoulders disappointedly.

Bennett and Cardigan spoke almost simultaneously, the latter's voice an instant later than his blond partner's.

"Damn, Cleve, that's an idea!"

"The *nitrosite!*" Cardigan exclaimed.

They both stopped abruptly, looked at the puzzled Torgan, and broke into exultant laughter.

"Lord, Cleve," Bennett said, "there's enough of the explosive in the shack by the *var-dust* cache to do the job!"

Torgan stared at them puzzledly, wondering how his wishful thinking aloud had helped.

"We can barricade ourselves in the tunnel leading to the *var-dust* underground supply stores," Cardigan said. "Make it look strictly last ditch defense. That small ridge across the center of the clearing around the *var-dust* cache will seem like a natural for them to select as a breastwork from which to pick us off. The ridge is within excellent range of the underground cache tunnel and they won't hesitate to line themselves up behind it for the siege."

Bennett nodded. "Perfect. And all we do is have the ridge mined with the *nitrosite* sticks, have the sticks fused in on a central charge wire which we set off from the tunnel entrance, once they're nicely grouped for the killing!"

"Brother," said Cardigan, you're talking lovely language. But let's get started. We'll have to work fast. We can't afford to post Torgan on watch along the trail, since we'll need his expert hand in covering up any trace of our *nitrosite* planting."

CHAPTER TEN

THE *var-dust* cache was located in a slightly smaller clearing some two hundred yards from the open area around the shaft and drill shacks of Eighty. It was accessible only through a thick jungle of *astera-tropical* Vegetation some fifty yards deep and three hundred yards long.

The cache itself lay at the far end of the clearing and consisted of an underground *duralloy*-constructed shelter sixty yards long and twenty yards wide. It had but one entrance and exit, that consisting of a sloping tunnel which ran from the surface of the clearing twenty feet down into the vault.

Lying less than fifty yards from the tunnel entrance—and almost directly in the center of the clearing—was the natural mud ridge breastwork in which Cardigan and Bennett had determined to plant the *nitrosite*.

Save for the squat shack in the far corner of the clearing where the *nitrosite* had been stored out of range of shaft blasting operations, the rest of area was open.

Cardigan, Bennett, and Torgan quickly emptied the squat shack of its *nitrosite* supply, carrying the boxes of the foot-length explosive charges directly to the mud ridge breastwork in the center of the clearing.

Bennett buried the charges as Cardigan wired them. Following behind their operations, Torgan cleverly removed all betraying traces of the planted explosives.

At length the minefield was laid, covering the entire length of the natural breastwork and an area of a dozen yards behind it. Cardigan unwinding the charged wire from the breastwork to the tunnel, Torgan followed along cunningly concealing the evidences of its presence.

The planting of the mine trap took almost half an hour, and when it was accomplished, Bennett, Cardigan and Torgan retired to a position in the mouth of the vault tunnel to wait.

The moments passed like separate eternities. Torgan, of the three, was the only one showing no impatience. He lay sprawled forward on the tunnel floor with Cardigan at his right and Bennett just beyond, moving not a muscle as he held his electra-rifle trained on the edge of the clearing through which the brigand band would be most likely to appear.

Cardigan cursed in a steady, almost inaudible monotone betraying his impatience and anxiety, while Bennett shifted his position again.

Finally, after more minutes, which were seemingly centuries, Torgan looked up from the sights on his electra-rifle to announce: "They coming."

Cardigan's cursing stopped abruptly. Bennett quit his restless shifting, and his lean, long body stiffened tautly. A minute passed, and then Cardigan and his partner were able to hear the sounds that Torgan had caught before them.

Voices, low and cautious, and the noise of bodies pushing through the thick jungle brush.

"They're at the edge of the drill shaft clearing," Cardigan whispered. "They'll be pushing through to this clearing in a minute or so."

THE voices were slightly more audible, but still indistinguishable, now, and definitely drawing closer with every instant. Then there was the sound of bodies moving through the underbrush once more, and Bennett exchanged glances with his partner.

"Open as accurate fire as we can from this distance the moment one of them pokes his head out of the clearing," Cardigan whispered. "If you can pick a couple off, so much the better. We want to make it seem like we're trying to keep 'em from gaining the breastwork."

"Right," Bennett muttered.

Torgan's grunt indicated pleasure at the suggestion.

The first of the brigands stepped from the brush into the clearing less than four seconds later.

Torgan's electra-rifle crackled, and the brigand, a short, swarthy man, dropped quickly to the ground, shouting something in sharp alarm.

"You're too high," Cardigan said. Torgan's grunt of disgust was drowned by sudden shouts from the underbrush as the rest of the brigand band piled out into the clearing and, hurling themselves to the ground, immediately opened an incredibly swift answering fire.

Both Bennett and Cardigan were firing as rapidly as possible, now, as the brigands poured forth from the jungle thickets. The air was electric with the crackling exchange of fire.

"Got one!" grunted Cardigan as a brigand stepped from the underbrush and pitched back into it with a sprawling, wide-armed lurch.

"Another!" Bennett exclaimed an instant later, as the first of the attackers tried to rise and sprawled face forward, arms out-thrust.

The fire from the brigand line suddenly ceased, the silence being shattered only by the electra-rifle crackling from the tunnel now.

"Hold it," Bennett snapped.

Torgan and Cardigan ceased firing.

"How many piled out?" Bennett asked. "I counted six."

"So did I," Bennett said. "As long as they keep their heads low we can't get any more from this range."

"There's four still in cover in the brush, then," Bennett declared.

In confirmation of his statement, a fresh burst of electra-rifle volleying started from the brush at the edge of the clearing.

"Low!" Cardigan snapped. Bennett and Torgan followed his example and hugged be tunnel floor. The fire from the electra-rifles crackled perilously close to their position.

"Cover fire," Bennett said, grimly satisfied, "while the four already out of the clearing make a dash for the breastwork!"

Cardigan grinned crookedly, reaching back to touch the charge switch on the mine plants lovingly.

"That suits me fine," he said. "I hope none of 'em stumbles."

"They've made the breastwork," Bennett reported a moment later, as he raised his head slightly again.

Electra-rifle fire began to crackle from the breastwork gained by the attackers, now, and it was just as effective in keeping Torgan, Cardigan and Bennett from response as the fire from the brush had been.

Cardigan lifted his head slightly.

"Another covering fire stunt," the reported. "The four from the brush are making a dash for the breastworks. There's a huge son-of-a-spacebum out in front of that dash. Damn—he's almost Torgan's proportions!"

CARDIGAN dropped back and reached for the switch that would throw the explosion charge on the *nitrosite* buried under the mud ridge breastwork.

"Take a peek," he grunted to Bennett, "and let me know the minute they're all lined up for the trip to hell. We can't run the risk of one of 'em getting wise from that range and tossing an atomic grenade into our tunnel. We gotta make this short and sweet."

"Hold it," Bennett snapped. "We aren't certain that there aren't any more of them. If there are, they'll pop out and line up with their pals behind the ridge in another few minutes. If there aren't, we'll know pretty quickly."

"Dammit, hurry!" Cardigan insisted.

The electra-fire from the breastwork ceased suddenly. Bennett raised himself on one elbow, peering forward.

"Just a few seconds longer," he cautioned Cardigan. "We'll know if there'll be others in a moment."

A voice coming from behind the mud ridge breastwork suddenly broke the silence.

"One chance," it boomed across to them. "Come out now, hands high, minus weapons. We want only the *var-dust*. You can save yourselves if you come out, hands high, now!"

"Sure, give it to 'em on a platter, and then end up with our heads on the same platter!" Cardigan snorted. "We'll do no coming out, but they certainly will, right now!"

"Damn it!" Bennett snapped. "Hold it a moment longer. There might be others. That proposition rings suspicious to me."

"But not suspicious enough to me," Cardigan growled. "Here they go—up in smoke!"

At that instant another voice rang out across the clearing. A voice eerily familiar to both Cardigan and Bennett.

"Stop!" the voice cried. "Cease this carnage!"

The three in the tunnel turned instantly in the direction from which this new voice came, turned to see the tall, gaunt, black-tunicked figure to whom the voice belonged striding out into the clearing from the far corner.

"My gawd—the Reverend!" Bennett gasped.

"Zender!" Cardigan exclaimed.

The tall, big-boned, awkward figure of the missionary was moving slowly, majestically, toward the breastwork of mud ridge shielding the brigands. Cardigan and Bennett exchanged sick, wordless glances as the missionary threw his long arms wide and boomed forth another command.

"Repent, ye spawn of the devil!" the Reverend Zender thundered. "Repent, before more blood stains your hands!"

The tall, somber-tunicked figure had acted almost hypnotically on both sides of the battle line, and the ridiculously booming pulpit-like commands had furthered the electric spell.

"They'll plug him soon as they believe their eyes and ears!" Cardigan whispered huskily. "I'd better throw the switch pronto!"

"You can't!" Bennett grabbed his partner's arm savagely. "He's in range of the explosion. It would blow him spaceward with the others!"

CARDIGAN'S lips moved wordlessly in silent profanity. He glared from Bennett back to the gauntly commanding figure of the Reverend Zender who had now paused less than ten yards from the mud-ridge breastwork and stood rigidly, arms still outstretched, facing the brigands.

"The damned fool!" Cardigan grated. "The crazy damned fool!"

"Good lord!" Bennett exclaimed hoarsely. "I think I know what the idiot is trying to do!"

"Trying to do—nothing," Cardigan rasped. "He's gone raving mad, I tell you. He doesn't know what he's doing!"

"Don't you see?" Bennett choked. "He thinks he's creating diversion enough to get us the hell out of this apparent trap in the tunnel mouth. He's giving us our only possible break to make a dash for the jungle fringe. The poor damned fool would naturally have no idea that we're holed up here by choice. He thinks he's making the great sacrifice!"

Cardigan's expression was one of futile rage.

"If he's bent on making himself a sacrificial pig, we might as well blow the works up right now!" he argued.

"No!" Bennett snapped. He raised himself on his elbows and started wriggling from the tunnel mouth.

"Stay here, you idiot!" Cardigan hissed. "You can't help him."

But Bennett was already beyond Cardigan's frantic reach for his legs, wriggling rapidly over the clearing toward Zender. The tall, gaunt missionary's distraction still held the attention of the brigands behind the mud-ridge breastwork for the moment, and they weren't aware of Bennett's sudden action as yet.

Neither was the Reverend Zender.

"Put down your arms!" he roared. "Put down your arms and end this carnage!"

An electra-rifle crackled suddenly, and the Reverend Zender toppled sideward to the ground. Cardigan turned to see Torgan, who had fired the shot at the missionary, methodically sighting his weapon for another blast at the man he'd downed.

"Torgan!" Cardigan hissed angrily.

The big Igakuroan turned an impassive green face to Cardigan. He looked surprised.

"Mission Boss in way; Torgan put out of way," he said. Then he added apologetically, "Only catch in leg. Better this time."

Cardigan grabbed the barrel of the weapon with one hand.

"Hold your fire," he whispered hoarsely.

Zender had fallen close by the front of the breastworks, and was apparently not seriously wounded. The missionary was trying to rise and having difficulty in doing so.

Bennett, at the sound of Torgan's shot, had stopped snaking forward toward the missionary, and now hugged the ground in the scant cover of a shallow ditch.

And then the brigand fire opened.

Cursing, Cardigan released his grasp on Torgan's gun and opened fire with his own rifle.

"All right," he shouted. "Fire now—at the one behind the mud ridge, not at the other two! Try to give Bennett Boss some sort of covering fire!"

CARDIGAN concentrated on seeking a target at any point along the breastworks, raking his fire evenly along the mud ridge in an effort to keep any of the brigands from exposing themselves long enough to draw an accurate bead on Bennett.

The crackling of fire and counter fire was an unbroken din, now; and Torgan, seeing Cardigan's method of fire, complemented it with a crossfire, working along from the opposite point of the breastworks.

Cardigan cursed volubly again, as he saw Bennett wriggle forward from the shallow ditch and continue toward the fallen Zender who, close to the edge of the mud ridge, was out of the brigand's line of fire.

But Zender had seen Bennett at last, and was dragging himself from his position of temporary safety. Dragging himself out toward the center of the clearing between the two battle lines, and ignoring Bennett's line of approach.

Cardigan continued to work his electra-rifle steadily back and forth along the top of the mud ridge, and Torgan kept up his counter directional fire.

Bennett had paused again, hugging the ground, on seeing Zender's strange reaction to assistance from him.

"That should teach the damned lunatic a lesson, if he lives through it," Cardigan snarled. "His heroic rescue is a dud, as far as that madman Zender's willingness to be rescued goes."

The crackle of electra-rifle fire continued unabated, and Zender was row almost equidistant between the tunnel mouth and the mud ridge breastwork.

Torgan stopped firing long enough to jab Cardigan's arm with his thumb.

"Maybe blow-up now," he suggested. "Bennett Boss and Mission Boss both out of bad-close distance."

For once Cardigan cursed himself. He had forgotten the mine switch completely in the ensuing excitement after Bennett had started for Zender. Profanely, Cardigan told himself so, while ordering Torgan to take up the fire again as he reached back for the switch.

Cardigan found the detonation switch and turned, wanting one last assurance that both Bennett and the wounded missionary were out of range.

It was then that he saw Zender rise lurchingly to his feet.

The missionary was apparently oblivious to the fact that he was exposing himself utterly to a blazing crossfire. He seemed only concerned in fumbling at his black tunic jacket in search of something inside it.

Jaw rigid, Cardigan watched, his hand still on the detonator. What in the hell was the madman doing?

And then Cardigan saw. Zender's hand came forth from his black tunic jacket holding a silver metal ball the size of a huge egg.

"Good lord!" Cardigan exploded, "An atomic hand grenade!"

The Reverend Zender let fly with the missile in the next instant. Let fly unerringly, hurling the missile into the center of the brigand breastworks.

THE explosion was immediate and deafening! The ground shook and smoke billowed whitely upward, obscuring the entire mud ridge. The shock of the burst threw Zender to the ground; and as Cardigan looked up again, the missionary took another atomic grenade from his tunic jacket and hurled it at what remained of the brigand defense works.

The second detonation was just as deafening as the first, and considerably more final in its results. There was nothing remaining of the mud ridge when the smoke cleared.

Bennett was on his feet, then, running toward the prostrate missionary. Cardigan, climbing from the tunnel, was followed by Torgan in a dash toward the same spot.

When they reached the missionary, Bennett had already assisted the Reverend Zender to his feet. The gaunt-faced man was dazed, and blood ran from his mud-smeared features, but he smiled weakly.

"I think that took care of them, gentlemen," he said.

"Your daughter?" Bennett asked.

"Where is your daughter?"

"She is safe," the missionary said. "Somewhere in the thicket fringes of the clearing."

Bennett went off instantly in the direction the missionary had indicated, leaving Cardigan and Torgan to help the Reverend Zender.

The missionary made a grimace of pain as he hobbled along between Cardigan and the huge native.

"I hope I didn't interfere with your plans too much, Mr. Cardigan," he said dryly.

Cleve Cardigan suddenly exploded.

With cold anger at first—anger ultimately giving way to searing rage—he told the missionary just how much and in what fashion he had interfered with the mine trap which had been set for the brigands. And as Cardigan lapsed into lurid verbal estimation of the interference, the Reverend Zender grew increasingly tight-lipped and white-faced.

Cardigan finished with: "And therefore, Zender, if you're pinning medals on yourself for your lunacy and luck, you know what you—'"

Torgan cut Cardigan off.

"But Cardigan Boss," he said puzzledly, "blow-up trap not work. You throw blow-up switch once and it not work."

Cardigan gaped at Torgan in astonishment.

"What in the hell are you talking about?" he demanded.

"When Mission Boss stand up to throw egg, I see your hand, Cardigan Boss, throw switch by mistake. I wait for blow-up. But blow-up not come. Not come until egg from Mission hit mud ridge."

"You mean I accidentally threw the switch just before he tossed the grenade?" Cardigan exploded. "You're crazy, Torgan. Why, if I threw that switch it would have made an instantaneous detonation of those mines and—" He paused, suddenly white-faced. "Just a minute," he said weakly.

Cardigan turned away and walked swiftly back to the tunnel entrance. He bent over the detonation switch box that had been left there. The switch had been pushed to "contact." He gulped, straightening up. Then a wire leading from the box to the tunnel edge caught his eye, and he saw why the detonator would never have exploded the mines. One of the sharp edges of the *duralloy* tunnel had somehow caught the wire and severed it.

Cardigan returned to the missionary and Torgan slowly. His face was crimson.

"Reverend," he said huskily, "I want you to do me a favor. I want you to use your kicking foot on my backside as soon as that leg of your heals again."

The Reverend Zender smiled.

"I'll be very glad to, Mr. Cardigan," he said...

CARDIGAN looked up as the Reverend Zender, leg swathed in bandages, limped onto the shattered veranda of a badly scarred compound many hours later. Cardigan had put away a quarter of the bottle of whiskey on the table before him, and was well on his way toward finishing off the rest.

The missionary took a seat across the table from the wide-shouldered young man.

"You mind, Reverend?" Cardigan asked uncomfortably, indicating the bottle on the table.

The missionary shrugged, smiling faintly.

"I didn't come here to convert you, Cardigan. I came to serve as a missionary for the natives."

Cardigan grinned. "That's good," he said. Then he added: "How's your daughter?"

"Just fine," said the Reverend Zender. "It is just as well she was unconscious in those thickets when I marched out to—ah—" he smiled wryly, "upset your plans. Otherwise, I'd have had trouble keeping her out of the thick of things."

"I take it, then, that she is stubborn," Cardigan said.

The Reverend Zender winced

"Even more than her mother was," he said. He smiled. "Yes, Carol is a very determined girl. Though few people realize it, she more or less rules me, you know."

"Is that so?" Cardigan said. He filled his glass, took a sip, sighed. "She's having Pete Bennett show her around the shambles of the wharfside at the moment, isn't she?"

The missionary nodded. "I think she has taken a fancy to young Mr. Bennett."

"Have a drink, why don't you?" Cardigan asked suddenly.

The Reverend Zender shook his head. "Frankly, I'd like to. I don't disapprove of a little now and then in—ah—moderation. But..." and his grin was suddenly wry, "...my daughter will not permit me to indulge."

Cardigan had a hard time keeping his face straight.

"Then she drastically disapproves?" he asked.

The missionary nodded.

Cardigan broke into a grin, which he could no longer conceal. He took a deep draught from his glass, put it down, and began to chuckle.

The Reverend Zender looked at him curiously.

Cardigan stopped chuckling and, still smiling, explained: "I was thinking of my partner, Pete Bennett," he said. "He has taken the same fancy to your daughter as she has to him. Supposing they're married?"

"They will be," said the missionary, smiling. "She told me she had decided to marry him, and she always has her way."

Cardigan's laughter was unrestrained. Between whoops he said, "Don't get me wrong. She's a beautiful girl. But Pete's habits are—well—as bad as mine. I was just thinking…how quick he'll have them changed."

The Reverend Zender's grin was wide.

"They will be changed so swiftly his head will swim," he promised. Then he sighed. "But I am looking forward to that marriage, young man. For you see, once Carol has young Bennett to boss, I'll gain my own freedom."

Cardigan broke into laughter, and this time the missionary joined him. They were still laughing as Pete Bennett and Carol Zender came up the veranda steps.

Neither Bennett nor the girl knew why…

THE END

If you've enjoyed this book, you will not want to miss these terrific titles…

www.ingramcontent.com/pod-product-compliance
Lightning Source LLC
Chambersburg PA
CBHW030324180626
46810CB00003B/1229